Mercy in Passion

Book Three of the Passion Series

SHIELA STEWART

Let the Romance
Capture your Heart
Shiela Stewart

MERCY IN PASSION
Book Three of the Passion Series

Cover art by Beverly Maxwell
ISBN Trade paperback: 978-1-60202-107-5
ISBN MS Reader (LIT): 978-1-60202-106-8
Other available formats (no ISBNs are assigned):
PDF, PRC & HTML

Linden Bay Romance, LLC
Palm Harbor, Florida 34684
www.lindenbayromance.com

First Linden Bay Romance publication: March 2008

To every woman who has ever loved a bad boy.
This one's for you.

Prologue

What the hell was he doing? This was wrong. It was criminal. He couldn't go through with it.

Justin took a step back while his best friend knelt down on the ground, jimmying the lock. He didn't want to break into the store. He'd thought Wes had been kidding, but when they'd arrived at the store, Wes had begun picking the lock.

He had to stop this before it went too far.

"I'm in."

Justin looked down at Wes, crouched on the ground, a wide grin on his face. He had to stop this. "We can't do this."

"What?" Wes stood, taking the flashlight from Justin.

"This isn't right. We shouldn't be doing this."

"What the fuck are you talking about? We agreed to do this; we planned it. And now you're getting fucking cold feet? Screw that, Justin." Wes gave the back door a shove then stepped over the threshold. "It's too late to stop now, my friend. The deed is done."

Justin's throat went dry when Wes stepped further into the shop. Sure, they'd talked about breaking into the local Gas 'N Gulp, but shit, it had been talk. How the hell had he gotten from talking about it to actually doing it? "I can't do it."

"Fuck you, man. You agreed. Now get your ass in

here and help me loot this place."

Justin took another step back. "I can't. You shouldn't be doing this either, Wes."

"Don't go getting all holier than thou on me now, man. Get the fuck in here and help me."

"No." Justin took a deep breath, then walked away.

"Don't you dare walk away from me, Justin. I swear, if you don't come back here and finish this, I'll beat your fucking head in."

Justin waved a hand at him and kept walking.

"You'll regret this, fucker," Wes spat at him in a low growling whisper.

No, he wouldn't regret it, but he would have if he'd followed through. Hearing the sirens of the police car in the distance, Justin quickened his steps.

Wes was going to be in deep shit now.

The house was quiet when he entered through the back door. His mother and sisters were away, visiting her parents for the week. Justin hadn't wanted to go along, though now, he regretted not doing so. Climbing the steps down to his bedroom, Justin thought about Wes. Had he been caught? Served him right if he had been. Idiot.

Climbing into bed, he dozed off the second his head hit the pillow. He was abruptly awoken not long after by his father looming over his bed, calling out his name.

"Wake up, Justin."

"I'm awake. What?" He rubbed tired eyes while sitting up.

"Where were you tonight?"

"Out. Why?" The light flicked on and he cursed. "Jesus, Dad, that's bright."

"What were you doing and who were you doing it with?"

Fuck. "I was just hanging with my friends. What's the big deal?"

"Were you with Wes tonight?" his father demanded.

Oh, shit. "No."

His father glared down at him with sharp blue eyes that always looked at him with disappointment. "You're lying to me."

"No, I'm not. What the hell is this all about?"

"Were you with Wes Donnelly tonight and did you have any part in breaking into the Gas 'N Gulp?"

Shit! Shit! "No!"

"Wes says differently."

"Well, he's lying."

"I don't think he is. I think you were with him tonight, and I think you took off the instant you heard the sirens."

Furious, Justin threw back the covers and stood. "You're always so quick to think the worst of me."

"You've given me no reason to think otherwise."

"Great, fucking great."

"Justin!"

"Whatever. Believe what you like. You won't listen to me anyway."

"Why should I when all that comes out of your mouth are lies."

"I'm not lying. Fine, I was with him, and yes, I was there when he broke into the place, but I didn't help him. I left before anything happened because I didn't want any part of that. But you don't believe me, as usual, so why bother." His father grabbed his arm so tight it actually smarted.

"I'm fed up with your lies, Justin, fed up with your behavior, and fed up with dealing with your crap all the time."

He shook his father's hand loose and snarled his response. "Fine, you're sick of dealing with me, then I'm out of here."

"What are you doing?"

He stuffed as many of his clothes and belongings into his duffle bag as possible. "Packing."

"Oh, so now you're just going to run away?"

"Yes." And he couldn't be happier.

"And where will you go?"

"Anywhere that's not here."

"You can't leave."

Justin squared his shoulders and glared at his father. "I'm eighteen, you can't stop me."

"Fine. Do what you like, but don't come crawling back home when you have no place to go and no money to live off of."

"Trust me, I won't." Justin slung the pack over his shoulder, shooting his father a nasty glare before walking past him. "Tell Mom I'll call." He stormed out of the house, vowing to never come back.

Chapter One

The sounds of heavy metal music blasted in the car, vibrating not only the speakers but the windows, as well. Beating his hands on the steering wheel to the drumbeat, he drove along the highway to his destination.

Passion.

Justin Davis was on his way home.

Oh, Lord!

The last time he'd traveled on this particular road, he'd been heading as far away from the town as possible. He'd vowed to his friends, on more than one occasion, that he'd only come back when Hell froze over. Looked like things were about to get chilly. Justin wondered what sort of reception he would get when people found out he'd returned. He hadn't exactly been a pillar of the community before he'd left. If there was trouble, Justin had been in the middle of it. He fancied his booze and he did what he could to prove to everyone he wasn't the sweet blond-haired, blue-eyed, good boy his looks implied. He liked to have fun and had done it as often as possible.

Man, he'd been an ass in his day.

But mostly when he'd been with Wes Donnelly.

Hammering his palms on the dashboard to the strong bass, Justin looked back at his past.

He'd been a good kid most of his life, up until Wes had come to Passion when Justin had been fourteen. Wes had been from the big city, and Justin had envied anyone who lived in the city. Not that he hated Passion; it was just too damn small and so often boring. The city had bright lights, lots of activity, and plenty of breathing room. So Justin had clung to Wes and every story he told of big city life.

Before Justin knew it, he was emulating his friend, including getting into trouble.

It had mostly been minor stuff: vandalism, rowdiness, drunk and disorderly conduct, fighting, disobedience. The instant Wes found out Justin's father was chief of police in Passion, he'd ribbed Justin about it every chance he got.

"Cop's son can't do no wrong with daddy looking after him," Wes had always said.

But Justin had proven him wrong. When he'd gotten in trouble, his father had been right there, breathing down his neck. Victor Davis claimed to love his son dearly, but wouldn't stand for his shit.

What choice had he had but to rebel? Justin was the stubborn type and so often butted heads with his father. The last thing Justin wanted was to follow in his father's footsteps, and he hated it passionately when he was compared to his father. He was his own person, yet no one seemed to recognize that.

Well, except for his friends, the Healys.

Living next door to Beth, Tyler, and Kevin had been great. Anytime you were bored, you could hop the short fence and drag one of them out for a quick game of b-ball or hockey or whatever else you could think of to do. Justin had thought of Tyler and Kevin like brothers, and Beth as his best pal. He had two of his own sisters; he hadn't needed another one. Beth was the oldest by two and a half years, he and Tyler were six months apart, and Kevin, the baby, two years younger.

He loved his sisters, Donna and Abby, dearly, but

having two younger sisters had often been a pain. So he'd latched on to the Healys. Sure, Beth was as female as his sisters, but she hadn't been a girly female. She loved getting dirty and playing as rough as the boys did.

His earliest memories ran back to constantly hanging with the Healy kids. He even considered their parents his aunt and uncle, though they weren't any relation what so ever. Victor Davis and Thomas Healy had grown up together and were life-long friends. Tom and his wife, Cassie, were a great pair, and Justin loved hanging at their house. Tom was a famous artist who was filthy rich and built like a wrestler. Cassie had her trinket shop on Main Street that did very well. It was his little secret, but he'd always had a tiny bit of a crush on his Aunt Cassie. She was a blond bombshell with a lovely personality.

His Uncle Tom had given him more than one talking to in his rebellious youth. Not that it did much good. Justin had still been a trouble-maker.

But he hadn't been a thief. That was where he drew the line.

His father hadn't believed him, no news there. Victor Davis rarely believed his son.

Sure, Justin gave his father cause to doubt him, but that last time, Justin had actually thought his father would trust him and believe that he hadn't taken part in the robbery.

Boy, had he been wrong.

Now here he was, on his way back, and why? Because he'd made a promise.

When he'd run away, his destination had been his grandparents' home in Mississauga. Justin knew his mother and sisters had been there, visiting. He thought he could go, hang out with them, maybe give his mother the sob story that his father had thrown him out, and she would take pity on him and give him some money so he could live on his own for a while.

It had been a nice plan, except... By the time he'd arrived, his father had already called ahead and informed them that Justin had left home. Of his own accord. Justin hadn't known that, though, when he'd shown up at his grandparents' home two days later, distraught and pleading with his mother for help, claiming his father kicked him out.

She'd let him have it like she'd never done before.

Normally his mother was a softy when it came to him. She always babied him and stood up for him. Not this time. This time she lit into him like a woman possessed. Man, had she been angry. And hurt. Hurt because Justin had tried to play her against her husband with a lie.

She'd left the next day, giving Justin an ultimatum. He either shaped up or he would not be welcome back home until he had.

That had shocked him and gave him pause for thought.

Then his grandfather had lit into him. And he hadn't been as kind. He'd told Justin it was time he acted like a man and did something with his life. "Stop being such an ass and grow up." And that had been the mild part of their conversation.

Justin had been so shocked that he had agreed to everything his grandfather had said, including getting a job and paying his own way in life.

The first job he'd gotten was as a busboy at a fancy restaurant.

He'd lived with his grandparents for a year before moving out on his own. His grandfather showed him how to invest his money wisely, and so Justin had. It didn't take long for his money to grow, and after two years of saving and investing, Justin opened his own nightclub.

Just In Time.

His parents knew how he was doing, not because he called them to tell them, but because his grandparents kept them apprised. Justin had still been smarting with both his parents.

Then six months ago, his grandfather had been

diagnosed with prostate cancer. Within weeks he was deathly ill and everyone knew he wouldn't make it. On his deathbed four weeks earlier, Leo Wilson had made Justin promise he would go home and smooth things out. Justin hadn't wanted to, but his grandfather had guilted him into it.

So here he was, heading home.

God help him.

Remnants of the winter's snowfall still lingered in the ditches along the road. Spring had sprung, but winter wasn't giving up the fight just yet.

The flash of police lights in his rearview mirror caught his attention. Checking his speedometer, Justin cursed heavily. Slowing down, he pulled to the shoulder and hoped it wasn't his father who was pulling him over. When he saw the officer step from the vehicle, he let out a long breath. It wasn't his father, unless he'd had a sex change. No, the officer approaching him was all woman. Tall, lean, and built like a goddess.

Pressing the button on his door, his window slid down, and he tilted his head towards the beauty before him. "Afternoon, Constable."

"You were speeding," she said in a deep, breathy growl that rang a bell in his mind.

"I know. Guess I wasn't paying attention to the speed." Her face was as stunning as her body was.

"Mind turning your music down?"

Damn, that voice was sexy. "Sure." He shut it off, then flicked the glove compartment door open and pulled out his license and registration. "I know the drill. Here you go." As he handed her his ID, he saw the name plate over her left breast. "Constable Healy. Beth?"

"Justin?"

"Yeah, it's me. Jesus, look at you, all copped out." Pushing his door open, he stepped out and had a good look at the woman he'd grown up with. "Holy hell, look at you." He swiped the hat off her head and whistled as all that blond hair tumbled free.

"Give me back my hat, Justin." She yanked it from his grasp, then pulling her hair up, slid the hat back in place.

He couldn't get over how much she'd changed. When he'd left she had been tall, thin, shapeless, with a short crop of blond hair. Now...well, she was gorgeous, complete with plenty of luscious curves. And she looked pretty hot in that uniform.

"You look incredible." But when he leaned towards her, ready to take her into his arms for a welcome hug, she pulled away.

"I see you haven't changed much. Still breaking the law." She pulled out her pad and began writing.

"What is that?"

"A ticket." She snapped it off and held it out to him. "Slow down."

Looking down at the paper in his hand, Justin chuckled. "Funny." He tore it in half, then looked up when she gasped. "What?"

"You can't rip up a ticket." She proceeded to write out another one.

"Give me a break, Beth." He took the second one and repeated his action with the first.

"Fine, have it your way."

She pulled out her handcuffs, and he looked down at them with bewilderment. "What the hell are you doing with those?"

"Cuffing you."

She spun him around so fast, he didn't have time to protest and the next thing he knew, she was slapping the cold steel onto his wrist.

"You have the right to remain silent—"

"You can't be serious." But when she yanked him up, and pushed him toward her cruiser, he got the feeling she was perfectly serious. "Beth, don't do this."

"You should have accepted the ticket. Watch your head," she advised, opening the door to the back of the cruiser.

He ducked as she shoved him into the car. "I didn't

think you were serious."

"I'm always serious when it comes to my job." She slammed the door then climbed into the driver's seat.

Apparently, she was. "What about my car?"

"It'll be towed to town."

"I didn't lock it up." He could just see it now, a beauty like his Porsche 911 wouldn't stay on the side of the road long unlocked. He jerked forward when she slammed on the brakes. What the hell was she doing now? When she backed the car up and stopped beside his, he was sure she'd come to her senses. Then she slid from the car and headed to his. She locked his doors, grabbing his keys before heading back to the cruiser.

"Happy?"

"Not particularly, no."

"Tough."

"Look, I'll pay for the ticket."

"Yes, you will."

His eyes narrowed in on the back of her head. A few tendrils of blond hair had escaped the hat. "I'd heard you'd become a cop. I had no idea you'd become a hard-ass."

"I'd watch what you say to me if I were you."

"*I'd watch what you say to me if I were you,*" Justin mimicked quietly. Sitting in the back of the police cruiser, he saw the sign as they approached Passion.

"Hasn't changed one bit," he grumbled, watching houses drift by while they drove, and when she stopped in front of police headquarters, his thoughts were only reinforced by the familiarity of the building before him. "Nothing's changed."

"Watch your head now," Beth advised, opening the door for Justin.

His eyes narrowed, he slid from the car. "You're enjoying this, aren't you?"

She simply took hold of his arm and led him towards the brick building.

They pushed through the door to the familiar scent

of strong coffee and cinnamon rolls. Millie, the receptionist and dispatcher, was still sitting behind the same desk at the front of the office. She hadn't changed much aside from a little more gray hair.

"Well, look what the cat dragged in."

"Complete with claws and a hiss," Justin nudged Beth with his arm but she failed to see the humor in his joke. "Hey, Millie, long time no see."

"Justin Davis. My, my, look at you. What a handsome man you've become."

So he was often told. "You're looking petty hot yourself. Lost some weight?"

"A little. So, what's our girl bringing you in for?" Her eyes shifted to Beth.

"Refusal to pay for a speeding ticket," Beth informed her.

"I didn't think she was serious," Justin proclaimed.

"He tore up two."

Millie clucked her tongue and shook her head. "Not smart."

"I didn't think she was serious," Justin insisted.

Millie shook her head. "Our girl is always serious when it comes to her work."

"So she told me," he muttered under his breath. "I said I'd pay the ticket." He heard the sound of the front door opening and, when he turned, saw his father enter the building.

"Would you look who just walked in," Millie announced, her voice sounding hollow in Justin's head.

His eyes caught those of his father, and once again, all Justin saw was disappointment.

Would things ever change?

"Hey, Dad."

Chapter Two

The silence that filled the space between them was a mile wide. Justin could well imagine what his father must be thinking right now. *Well, the bastard finally came home.*

"Justin."

And there was that silence again.

They'd practically said as much a month ago at his grandfather's funeral.

"I brought him in for refusing to accept the speeding ticket I wrote out to him," Beth piped in, breaking the silence.

"I didn't think she was serious." How many times did he have to say that? "I'll pay the damn ticket."

"Millie, write up the file."

"Will do, Chief."

It was nothing new for Justin when his father walked past him without even batting an eye. *Oh yeah, he was ready to make amends.* "What's the damage?" Justin asked, giving his attention to Millie. He was going to do his best to ignore the hurt he felt.

"You want me to fine him just for speeding, or for refusal to comply?" Millie asked Beth.

"Just the damn ticket." Beth shot him a nasty glare.

"It's my lucky day. Hey, you wanna remove these now?" Justin held his hands up, still cuffed in the steel. With a snarl on her face—and what a pretty face it was, Justin thought—she obliged. And not with an ounce of compassion, either. "You're too kind," he grumbled while rubbing his sore wrists.

"I'll be on patrol if you need me," Beth told Millie, then stomped out of the building.

"Isn't she Mary Sunshine? Okay, Millie, hit me with the damage." He paid the fine, which wasn't all that bad, gabbed a bit with Millie while she filled out the receipt, then headed to his father's office. "Send in reinforcements if you hear shots fired." Taking a deep breath, he raised his fist and knocked on his father's door.

"Enter."

Taking another deep breath, Justin pushed the door open and was hit with a blast from the past. The office was still the same. The large metal desk was still near the back and facing the door, one filing cabinet to the right and a window to the left. Two chairs were placed in front of the desk, and his father sat behind it. The palm tree his mother had brought to the office eight years ago had grown some, but looked a little sickly.

"Love what you've done with the place." Justin took one of the chairs. "So…."

"Did you pay the ticket?"

Straight to business. "Yep. I really didn't think Beth was seriously writing me up a ticket."

"Were you speeding?" his father asked soberly.

"Yes, but—"

"Then what made you think you wouldn't get a ticket?"

"We used to be friends."

"Friendship or not, an infraction is an infraction. What are you doing here?"

His father seemed stiffer than usual. And sitting this close to him, Justin could see his fifty-plus age showing in his face. His hair was still blond and cut short around a handsome face. But there were more wrinkles, especially at the corners of his blue eyes. "I was in the neighborhood and thought I'd pop in for coffee." When all his father did was stare at him with a blank expression, Justin cut the humor. "I made a promise to

Grandpa that I'd come home and make amends."

"So you do it by breaking the law?"

Here we go again. "I wasn't paying attention to my speed."

"Have you seen your mother yet?"

Look, I really don't want to be here either, buddy. "Not yet. She was going to be my first stop, but, well…things happened."

"Then I suggest you head over there now. She'll be leaving for work soon."

His mother worked at the local eatery and had for a number of years now. "I guess I'll get going, then." He knew when he wasn't wanted, always had. "Catch you around."

Justin left the office feeling much the same as he had years before. Glad to be gone.

~

There it was, his boyhood home. Two stories high, it was still white with brown trim with a white picket fence around the property. There were plenty of memories here. Good and bad. Barbeques in the summer, snowball fights in the winter. Christmases, birthdays, Thanksgivings, incredible food, lots of presents, and plenty of fun.

And then there were the bad.

Arguments, fights, silent treatments, and bitter words.

Shrugging them all off, Justin walked to the front door. It felt weird to knock, but it wasn't his home any longer and hadn't been for six years.

When the door opened and his mother answered, he held his breath. "Hi."

She looked up at him, her soft green eyes drinking in her son. "Hi, yourself."

They'd seen each other a month ago, and they'd been civil, more so than he and his father had been. But there was still tension. "I straightened out my life, can I come in?"

She stepped aside.

That was a good sign, and he could admit to himself that he'd worried she'd close the door in his face rather then let him in.

Not much had changed on the inside of the house, either. Had he expected it to change? Maybe a little. The living room was still set up the same, with the same cocoa brown sofa and chair and the family pictures still lining the fireplace mantel. The scent of food—probably from lunch—was still prominent in the air. "I was told you don't have much time before you have to head to work. Got ten?"

His mother shut the door and nodded. "I've got that. Want a drink or something?"

"I'm fine. You look good." His mother was not a stunning beauty, but she was beautiful. She had short, red hair that framed a delicate face that still looked as young now as it had years before. If she ever gained an ounce, he'd never seen it. She was, and probably always would be, stick thin.

"So do you. Come, sit." She led him to the sofa and they sat down, each on one end. "When did you get into town?"

"About half an hour ago. Beth brought me in. I was speeding," he explained.

"Oh, Justin," she sighed.

"It was stupid, I know, but I wasn't paying attention—" He shook his head. "Let's not get into that. I saw Dad." He watched her face for a reaction.

"And…?"

Didn't get one. "I live to tell the tale. It was short, not sweet, and, well…now I'm here."

"How long will you be staying?"

"Not sure yet. I guess it depends on you and Dad."

"So you're keeping your promise to your grandfather."

Justin cocked his head to the side. "How do you know about that?"

She shrugged, picking some unseen lint from the arm of the sofa. "Grandma told me. Are you serious about this? Because if you're not, get back in your car and go home."

His heart felt that statement with a heavy thud. "Well, nothing like feeling the love."

She took his face in her hand and tilted it up. "I do love you, baby. I have and always will love you. But you have to make an effort to change, to fix what's wrong and want to fix it." She laid her hand on his heart. "Truly want to fix it. Because if you don't really want this, then all you're doing is hurting those that love you most." She kissed his cheek, then stood. "I have to go to work. You're welcome to stay here while you're in town."

"I don't think that's a good idea." He stood with his mother and walked to the door, feeling like someone had cut out his heart. And when he climbed behind the wheel of his flashy red Porsche, Justin actually contemplated heading back home and forgetting about making amends.

Then he saw Beth strolling down the sidewalk, and he halted his plans momentarily. Slipping from the car, Justin leaned against the hood and waited. Damn, she looked hot in that uniform.

"Fancy meeting you here." She barely looked up at him before heading to her parents' house. Sliding off the hood, he hurried towards her. "Hold up," he pleaded when she kept walking. "Beth, wait up."

She spun around, stopping short, and he nearly rammed into her. "What?"

"Hi." He flashed a wide grin, only to have her pivot and walk away. Letting out an exasperated breath, Justin went after her. "Come on. What's your deal? Why are you pissed at me?" She spun on him again, only this time he was prepared for it. But not the cold stare she shot back at him.

"Why am I pissed? Got a year? No, you don't," she interrupted him when he opened his mouth to speak. "Because you'll be out of here before sunset and back to your own little world, forgetting about all the people you left behind."

She stomped up the stairs to her home, and he hurried after her, nearly losing his nose when she slammed the door in his face. "Jesus, Beth." As he'd done so many times in his past, he simply opened the door, feeling right at home, and followed her inside. "Will you just stop for one second and talk to me. Oh, hi, Uncle Tom. What's shaking?"

"Go away, Justin," Beth barked at him, then darted down the hall to her room.

"Hello, Justin," Uncle Tom finally said, standing to greet Justin with an outstretched hand.

"Sorry to just barge in." He took his uncle's hand in a solid shake. "Man, you haven't changed one iota. You're still as big as a house. Did I ever tell you how much I envied your muscles?"

"A few times. When did you get back?"

"An hour ago. Great to see you again." Darting down the hall, Justin didn't bother to knock on Beth's bedroom door and threw it open.

"What the hell are you doing?" she screeched, pulling her shirt against her breasts. "Get out!"

"Sorry. Damn, sorry," he repeated, shutting the bedroom door with a snap. Leaning against the wall next to her room, Justin let out a long breath. That had been quite the sight to behold, however brief it had been. When she threw the door open and stomped out, he bolted right after her. "Damn it, Beth, just talk to me." He grabbed her arm and what happened next totally shocked him.

Not to mention knocking him flat on his ass.

She sucker punched him right in the nose.

"Elizabeth!" his uncle hollered, rushing to Justin.

"He had it coming," she justified.

"Grab a damp cloth and some ice," he ordered her, then knelt down in front of Justin. "You okay, son?"

"Been a while since I've been knocked silly. Yeah, I think I am." He wasn't about to admit his face throbbed like a bitch and he was seeing stars. "I think she's pissed at me."

"What was your first clue?" Beth snarled at Justin, then handed her father the ice and cloth. He barely had it in his hands when she stomped through the room and left the house.

"Yep, she's pissed at you." His uncle nodded, pressing the cloth to Justin's nose.

Justin hissed through his teeth, not from the cold but from the pain. "Damn, she has a tough fist."

"Yeah, she does." Tom grinned like a proud father.

"So, what's new in your life?"

"Became a grandfather." He dabbed at the blood under Justin's nose.

"No shit. Beth?"

"Tyler."

"Ty has a kid?"

"And a wife."

"Jesus," Justin hissed again when Thomas laid the ice back on his nose. "When did all this happen?"

"A year ago. Tommy's three months old."

"Tommy?" Justin smiled. "Names his first son after dear old dad. Must make you proud?"

"It really does." Tom beamed.

"What about Kevin?"

"He's going to university in the city, comes home on the weekends."

"And Beth? Besides being pissed at me." He never expected her to sucker punch him in the face. Sure, in their youth they'd slugged each other in the arm now and then, but it was a far cry from getting slammed in the face.

"Still single and living at home. Well, I stopped the bleeding, but you'll have a shiner."

"Been a while since I had one. Adds to my charm. Thanks a bunch, Uncle Tom."

"Anytime. Good to have you back, Justin."

With a nod, Justin left the house. He'd give it time to see if he was glad to be back.

~

Her fist was throbbing like a son of a bitch and she regretting popping Justin in the face. But damn it, he just brought the nasty out in her. And really, she should give herself credit for waiting so long to do so. There'd been several opportunities since she'd first seen him that she could have popped him. He should be lucky she held herself back for so long.

Damn it, why had she hit him?

She'd promised herself not to care if he ever returned. Yet...

Why was he home now? Why did he have to look so damn good? Why did he have to affect her the way he did?

Why? Why? Why?

Agh! She was going to rip her hair out.

"Afternoon, Officer Healy."

"Afternoon, Miss Della. Lovely day we're having." Beth smiled at the elderly woman as they met on the sidewalk.

"That we are. You enjoy it while it lasts." Miss Della waved as she departed.

"I will. Have a nice day." She waved back and the sting in her knuckles reminded her of her fury.

Justin was damn lucky she only popped him once.

Six years was a long time to not see someone you once called your best friend. It had taken every ounce of willpower she had not to throw her arms around him when she'd pulled him over on the highway. Maybe if she hadn't been on duty, she might have—no, she still wouldn't have. Her pride wouldn't have allowed it.

She would not let him know how much she missed him. The louse deserved to be in pain right now. He'd done nothing but cause her pain for the past six years. It was time he felt some of what she was feeling.

She just wished he felt the ache in his heart like she felt in hers.

Hands in her pockets, Beth walked the streets of the town she called home.

Heartsick.

~

He had a mound of paperwork to go through and about a dozen emails to read, but Vic sat simply staring at his computer screen. His mind, obviously, was not on his work.

His only son was back, and he wasn't too sure what to think about it.

Vic knew he was doing well for himself. He and Julia had been kept up to date on their son, thanks to Julia's parents. Justin owned a night club and was making enough money to live more than comfortably. And, he'd stayed out of trouble.

But the reason for him being home was what bothered Vic. A promise to his dying grandfather, but did Justin actually mean to make amends, or was he simply fulfilling part of his promise in hopes it would appease his own conscience.

Time would tell, he supposed.

"Daydreaming?"

Vic looked up and saw his wife standing in the doorway, a smile bright on her lips. She was his light, his world, and he loved her as much now, if not more, than he had when they'd married twenty-five years ago. "Only of you, doll."

"You'd better be. Busy?"

"Oh yeah." He shut his computer down and stood to take her into his arms. "But it can wait. Aren't you supposed to be at work?"

"I'm on a break. Our son is home."

He held her, just savoring the feel of her. "Yes, he is."

"You think he'll stay longer than tonight?"

"Not sure. He come by to see you?" he asked, releasing her to sit on the edge of his desk.

She nodded while she took the chair. "I didn't have long to visit with him, though. If he's still here tomorrow, I was thinking of having a family meal. Would you be up for that?"

"I'm up for it if you are."

"I want him to stay home for good, but I know that's not going to happen. Hell, I want so much of what I can't have."

"Like a normal son who didn't run away from his problems and stayed home to be with his family?"

She nodded solemnly. "He's doing better for himself, but…"

"You have to wonder if he's sincere in why he's here."

"Yeah. I'm a bad mother, but I just don't know if I can trust him."

Vic stood and took hold of her hands. "Doll, stand in line. You're not the only one."

~

Well, here he was, back in Passion and staying in a crummy hotel. The last time he'd rented a room in the Passions Inn had been the night of graduation when he'd convinced Leanne Monroe to let him ease her out of her virginal burden. They'd been dating for three months and Lea had promised she'd sleep with him when they graduated. She kept to her promise, though it hadn't been the greatest experience. The first time never was. For women at least. But he'd shown her how beautiful the act of lovemaking could be plenty of times after that. Then she'd dumped him for a city boy and Justin never saw her again.

He'd left shortly after that anyway, so it all worked out.

Dropping his bag on the bed, Justin looked around the room. It consisted of one queen-sized bed draped in a horrible hue of pea soup vomit which matched the drapes. One round table sat near the window with two chairs beside it, and the twenty-inch TV on the rustic looking dresser looked like it had been there since he'd brought Leanne to the room six years ago. Stepping into the washroom, he noted that nothing much had changed here, either. Dull white walls with a yellow marble sink, and a mustard colored tub and toilet. At least it was clean.

Pulling out a drawer, he laid his clothing inside, then hung up the shirts he didn't want wrinkled. He tossed his bag in the closet, then stripped out of his black leather jacket and hung it over a chair.

Home sweet home.

Grabbing the remote, Justin made himself comfortable on the bed, then picked up the telephone book to look for take-out delivery. Thank God they still had the same pizza place. Vinnie's Pizza Palace had had phenomenal pizza before he'd left. He just hoped they hadn't changed their recipe in his absence.

Dialing the number, Justin ordered a large loaded and a bottle of Coke to go. They told him it would be half an hour, so now all he had to do was wait. Clicking on the TV, Justin flipped through the pathetic fifteen channels the hotel allowed their guests to view and waited for his pizza.

An hour later, having filled his belly, Justin clicked the TV off. There wasn't anything worth watching on TV.

Grabbing his jacket, Justin decided to head to the bar.

Chapter Three

He'd never been in the Pit-Stop before. Pushing through the doors, Justin groaned at the country music pumping from the speakers. His first thought was to turn and walk back out. But he wanted a beer, and he didn't want to drink it alone in his hotel room like a loser.

It was much better to drink it alone in a bar like a loser.

He took a table near the dance floor simply so he could watch for any hot chicks that might be willing to be seduced with some sweet talk and a cold drink.

"What'll you have?"

Justin looked up at the saucy looking redhead with eyes the color of ocean water and smiled. "A taste of you would be nice, but I'll settle for whatever you have on draft."

"You look familiar. Have you been in here before?"

"Not before today." He gave her his most charming smile, the one he knew all the women melted over. Unfortunately, she simply turned her back on him and walked away.

Couldn't win them all.

The place was jumping, for a small town hole-in-the-wall that played country music. He'd never been into that country-bumpkin-dump-your-lover-but-cheat-on-her-first, kinda music. Give him the hard pumping rock that sunk right into your core and made you want to take up the strings. That was what he played at his establishment.

"Here you go." The redhead set the mug of frothy beer on the table in front of him.

"Thank you, sweetheart." He wasn't getting to her even with all his charm.

Justin sat in the dimly lit bar, watching the couples two-step and line-dance to the music blasting on the jukebox. God, he hadn't been away that long, yet he couldn't believe how much he missed being at home in his own bar, where the music was loud and thumping, and the girls were happy to give you their time and their bodies.

"Holy shit. J.D. Is that you?"

Only one person had ever called him that, and when Justin looked over and saw Wes Donnelly looming over him, he thought for a minute that things might start looking up. "Well, hell. Wes Donnelly. Long time no see." He stood and held his hand out to his old friend.

By the time he saw the fist Wes held up to him, it was too late. The hard boney flesh connected with his right eye with a blinding force that sent Justin stumbling back and onto the table behind him.

"Watch it, buddy," the guy at the table he'd crashed into called out, then gave Justin a shove.

Justin stumbled and tried to right himself only to have Wes come at him with another fist. He managed to duck before that one hit him, but the guy who'd shoved him hadn't been as lucky. He took the fist to his face and knocked him out cold.

"Jesus, Wes. What the hell is your problem?" he managed before Wes came at him swinging.

"Break it up!" someone shouted as Justin took Wes down onto the floor.

"You got away with it, you fucker, and left me to twist in the wind."

Justin took the head slam like any person would, with a crack. His eyes flashed with bright colorful lights as the pain exploded inside his head. The next thing he knew, he was being hoisted up by the collar and pulled away. The room began to spin and Justin had a monetary thought that he might just embarrass himself and black out.

Then it all went black.

He woke however long after to a cold sensation on his face and bright blue eyes glaring down at him.

"He's coming back."

"Beth?"

"How many fingers you see, Justin?" she asked, holding up her hand.

"Three. I'm surprised that you didn't just hold up the middle one to me."

"He's good to go, boys." She stood up, giving her t-shirt a tug.

"What the hell?" Was Justin's response when he was hoisted up and handcuffed by two rather burly looking officers?

"We're taking you in for questioning in the matter of causing mischief, destruction of property, and causing bodily harm." One of the officers explained while Justin was walked outside.

"Me? What about Wes? He started it." The wind had a fair bite to it, and Justin felt it slice into his open wounds with a stinging force. Sliding his tongue over his bottom lip, he tasted blood. Great, another wound.

"He's being detained, too. Watch your head now."

In pain and righteous fury Justin sat in the back of the police cruiser with complete silence, the air around him swirling. He'd been inside a cruiser twice in one day. And he hadn't even been in town twenty-four hours yet.

Welcome fucking home.

It was a short drive, a whole two blocks to cop central, and when the officers pulled him out of the car, his head was pounding something fierce.

"Put him in cell two."

Justin glared at the young man behind the desk

while he was pushed forward. *Who the hell was that*?

"Here we go. You just sit tight now while we fill out some paper work and talk with the witnesses."

The handcuffs were removed, but they left him locked in a jail cell, which didn't make his day at all. "I'm injured here. I could use some compassion," he called out in an angry tone. Damn, his head was killing him, and everything had a double film on it, like he was partially crossing his eyes.

"You're fucking lucky you're still alive, Davis."

Looking out of the corner of his eyes, Justin saw Wes in the cell beside him. Great. He decided it was best just to ignore the prick.

"What, now you're too fucking good to talk to me?"

"Hey, you're the one that came at me. I *was* glad to see you before the five-finger welcome."

"Yeah, I bet."

"What the hell is your deal?" Justin snapped, glaring at Wes through the bars that separated them.

"You, you're my deal. Fucker."

When Wes turned his back on Justin, he simply shrugged and looked to the front of his cell. "Hey, can I at least get some fucking painkillers here?" He wasn't sure if he was glad or not to see Beth when she strolled up to the bars.

"You look like hell," she stated, then slid her hand through the bars. "Here."

Justin looked down and saw the pills in her palm. "Cyanide?"

"Something for the pain. And here's some water to wash them down." She slid the tiny cup through the bars.

He took both and downed the pills, chasing them with the water. "Thanks."

"I sent for Doc Williams to check you out."

"Be still my heart, what will I do with all this kindness you're showing me?" he stated sarcastically. She narrowed those big blue eyes at him, and Justin remembered all the times in the past when she'd done the very same thing. "You've still got gorgeous eyes."

"In case you're wondering, I saw the whole ordeal."

"Great! Wait, you were there? How come I didn't see you?"

"You were too busy ogling the women, which is nothing out of the norm. Over here, Doc," Beth called out and waved a hand in the air. She unlocked the door, and let the doctor into the cell.

His hair was graying at the temples, and he was tall, thin and looked like he'd spent too much time in the sun. Justin remembered the doctor from his youth when he'd seen him on a regular basis for his annual check-ups.

"Well, look at you, son, you certainly have grown. Nasty looking face, though." Taking Justin's chin is his hand, he clucked his tongue he examined it.

"It used to be stunning. Tell me it'll get back there after the bruising goes down?" He really didn't want a scar on his face. Women loved his face, and so did Justin. Even though he looked just like his father.

"With proper care, it should be back to normal in no time. Hmm, lip's split. Could use a stitch. Good thing I brought my kit."

"You're going to stitch me up in here?" Justin asked with surprise, looking down at the bag the doc perched beside him on the bed.

"Won't take but a minute and shouldn't be more than three stitches. Beth, honey, you wanna let me out so I can wash up and prep?"

"Sure thing, Doc." She let him out, then locked the door after him.

"If you saw what happened, then why am I behind bars?" Justin asked Beth. He didn't want to think about what was going to happen to him when the doc returned.

"Because you're a guilty bastard," Wes spouted snidely.

"Fuck you, Wes."

"You're here until everything is wrapped up and all parties have been questioned on the matter," Beth interrupted.

She sounded so damn professional. "He came at me, I was only protecting myself."

"Aw, damn."

Justin shifted only his eyes to his father as he walked up beside Beth. There was that disappointed look again. "Why are you here? Wait, they called you to tell you your son, the delinquent, was in jail, right?"

"What happened?" his father asked Beth, ignoring what Justin had just said.

"Wes clocked Justin, fight ensued."

"He came after me. I was only protecting myself."

"That's right, put the blame on someone else so daddy will bail you out. Again," Wes snarled.

Justin simply sent Wes the finger before responding to his father. "I was minding my own business, enjoying a beer, when Wes came up and clocked me in the face. He came at me again, hitting someone behind me, then charged at me one more time. I took him down, but it all went a little fuzzy after that." And his throbbing head told him it hadn't been pleasant.

"He's a little banged up," Doc Williams spoke, walking up beside his father and Beth. "I was about to stitch his lip."

Beth let him in and he walked right to Justin and took his chin. "Pupils are dilated, and since he blacked out, I would say mild concussion. Now, let's get this lip fixed up. This eye looks old, though."

Justin looked up at Beth with a sneer. "That one was courtesy of your local law official earlier this afternoon."

"You hit him?" his father asked with a choked expression.

"He pissed me off. I wasn't on duty," she justified.

"And that makes it better?" His father simply shook his head.

"Okay, gonna feel a bit of a prick here, then your

lip will go numb, and I'll get to work."

"I hate needles." Just the thought of them made Justin's skin clammy.

"I remember. Beth, you wanna come in here and watch him while I stitch him up?"

She unlocked the cell door and sat down beside Justin on the cot.

"Two kind gestures in one day. Pinch me, I think I'm dreaming. Ouch!" he yelped when she pinched his arm. Then he hissed out a breath when the doc grabbed his lip and sent the needle into the flesh. "Fuck," he mumbled and was damn glad when the needle slid free. "I don't really need it stitched up."

"Don't be a baby," Beth taunted.

"Easy for you to say. You're not the one with the cut lip. Oh hell, my mouth is going numb." And, damn, did it feel weird.

"Few more minutes and this will be all done. You need to keep some ice on that eye and that chin, and I suggest you set your alarm and wake yourself up ever two hours."

"Why?" Justin questioned and felt his stomach swirl when he saw the needle come up into view.

"You're concussed. Wouldn't want you dropping off into never-never-land for good. Here we go now."

His entire body tensed up, and he closed his eyes, expecting to feel a great deal of pain. He was more than a little surprised when all he felt was a slight tugging.

"You should see the size of that needle, J.D. Holy shit, is it long. Damn, it's going in real deep."

Justin knew Wes was taunting him, but damn, he was doing a good job of it. In his mind's eye, Justin could see a huge ass needle that looked like the length of his arm, slide into his lip. The swirling in his stomach intensified.

"There we go. All done. You keep this clean, now, and watch for infection. Come see me in a week and I'll remove the stitches. Catch you later." The doctor gathered up his stuff then stepped out when Justin's father unlocked the door.

Justin opened his eyes and tried to look down at his lip. "How bad does it look?" He couldn't feel his lip, which he figured was a good thing. At least a part of him wasn't in pain.

"Like hell," Beth said bluntly.

"Gee, thanks. So, how long do I have to sit in here?"

"Charges have been dropped," Constable Millar stated, opening the cell door.

"What?" Wes shouted, grabbing hold of the bars between them. "That's fucking bullshit."

"Witnesses all say Wes came after you, so you're free to go," Constable Millar informed Justin.

"See, daddy comes in and bails you out. Fucking typical."

"You're free to go, too, Wes. But you're on probation, and you'll pay the fine."

"Son-of-a-bitch!"

"I can't wait to get the hell out of here." And the sooner the better, Justin thought.

"The cell, or Passion?" Beth inquired, following Justin from the cell.

"The cell, though my homecoming hasn't exactly been a walk in the park; I'm not leaving yet. Damn, room's spinning." Like he was on a carousel, and it was not a fun experience.

Beth caught him on one side while his father took the other.

"I'll give him a lift to his hotel," Beth stated.

"I have my own car. Shit, it's still at the bar." He really didn't like how the room was spinning.

"Give me your keys, and I'll drive it back for you," his father insisted, holding out his hand.

With shaky hands, Justin fumbled in his coat pocket for his keys. "Be gentle with her."

His father snorted then took the keys and headed out. "What am I looking for?"

"Red Porsche 911."

"Damn. Nice car."

"And then thome. Damn, tongueth gone numb."

"Let's get you out of here." Taking him by the arm, Beth walked him out.

"Whath with the nith act. Damn it." He felt like such a fool, slurring his words.

"Maybe I feel guilty for knocking you flat earlier. This is my car."

Justin slid into the white Acura, glad to be sitting. "You thoud. Fuck! Why the hell ith my tongue numb?"

Beth snickered as she slid behind the wheel, then started them on their way. "Doc must've given you a bit too much freezing."

"Great." He sat back and closed his eyes, hoping to stop the swirling before his eyes.

"Justin?"

"What?" he jerked awake, his eyes wide.

"You fell asleep."

"I did not." Yet when he looked at the hotel before him, he couldn't remember getting here.

"Right. Where's your room key?"

"My pocket. I can manage it." But climbing from the car, he felt his legs shaking.

"Whoa there." She caught him when he staggered.

"The air moved on me."

"Sure it did. Which pocket?"

"Left." He felt her hand slid into his pocket and grope for the card. "I like your hair like thith." And with her leaning over him the way she was, he could smell the lovely apple blossom scent. "Itth longer."

"Yeah, decided to grow it out. Okay, here we go."

She led him to his door, and Justin heard the squeal of tires come to a halt behind him. As he turned, he saw his father step from his car.

"Nice car." His father beamed.

"Jealith? How long before thith thuff wearth off?"

"Probably an hour. You should stay at the house tonight, so we can keep an eye on you," his father stated, holding the keys out to Justin.

His father's words shocked him. He never expected that sort of kindness, not just in the offer, but in the way it was handed out.

"I'll stay with him and make sure he's okay," Beth offered, unlocking his room door.

"You will?" Another shock. If this kept up he was going to start thinking they both actually cared about him.

"Okay, then. I'll check on you tomorrow." His father shoved his hands in his pockets and walked away.

"Come on, let's get you inside and horizontal."

"You couldn't have said anything better. Jesus, my head is killing me." Justin sat down on the bed, glad to be off his feet, then fell back onto the pillows. "Heaven."

"I'll get some ice, and once I get it on your head it'll start feeling better."

"Works for me." He stayed where he was, closing his eyes to the pain when Beth left the room to get some ice.

"Justin."

"What?" His eyes flew open and he saw Beth standing over him. "Were your eyes always this blue?"

"Yes. You fell asleep while I was gone."

"Well, my head hurts, and I'm a little burnt out, so yeah, I guess I did." And it would be nice if she'd quit waking him up when he fell asleep. At least he could forget the pain while he was sleeping.

"I have the ice. Here." She put the towel filled with ice on his head and he sighed.

"Nice."

"Mind if I turn on the TV? I'll keep it low so it doesn't hurt your head."

"Sure, fine. I think I'll die now." He closed his eyes and wished away the pain.

~

Beth pulled up a chair and flicked on the TV, cranking down the volume immediately. She glanced over and saw that Justin had closed his eyes. She'd give him an hour, then wake him to make sure he was okay.

He was home. Justin had come home.

And he still made her heart throb.

She had so hoped to have gotten over him in his time away, but her love for him hadn't diminished in the six years since he'd run off. Now he was here, and she didn't know what to do about it.

She was angry at him for leaving. Hurt that he never once called her. Confused because she wanted nothing more than to lie down beside him and will the past six years away.

Turning back to the TV, she watched an old game show with about as much enthusiasm as a person getting root canal. Bored, she clicked it off and walked to the window. The weatherman had called for rain overnight. Great, with the chilly temperatures it was sure to turn to ice, which meant accidents on the highway. She wasn't on duty tomorrow, but if she was needed, she'd go in and help. She usually did anyway. She loved her job, loved being a cop, even though she'd only been one for less than four years. And only two of those had been in Passion. She'd been posted in another small town just down the road before being transferred to Passion. She preferred policing her hometown.

Leaving the window, Beth glanced down at Justin and stood there a moment, just watching him sleep. He was still so damn beautiful. Oh, she knew men hated being referred to as beautiful, but there was no other way to describe Justin. He had the face of an angel, eyes that were a sky blue with long, blond lashes. His mouth was full and, when he smiled, dimples formed at the corners. She'd always dreamt of kissing those dimples.

Yeah, he had the face of an angel, but the persona of the devil. Justin had loved pushing the limit in his youth, and truth be told, Beth had found it attractive, to a point. He was a bad boy, and what woman didn't love a bad boy?

She had. She did.

Sighing, Beth reached down and began removing his shoes. He was out cold, and she worried about him being unconscious until she began pulling his jacket off.

"Whatreyoudoing?" he slurred

"Taking your jacket off," she informed him, pulling his arm from one sleeve. It was a nice leather jacket and she wondered how much it had cost him.

"Oh yeah, undress me baby."

"Go back to sleep, Justin" She smiled, tugging his other arm free.

"Night, Beth."

"Goodnight, Justin. Roll over for me, okay?" When he rolled to his right, she gave him a nudge to the left. If she'd let him roll to his right, he would have fallen right off the bed. She tugged the jacket free, then grabbed the blanket from the opposite side of the bed and threw it over him. Since he was laying on it, she couldn't cover him completely, but it would do, she hoped.

She sat on the other side of the bed, propping the pillows behind her, then set her watch for one hour. Grabbing the remote, she clicked the TV on and flipped through the channels.

Chapter Four

Justin woke to the loud hammering inside his head, and when he opened his eyes, the sunlight streaming in through the thin excuse for curtains on the window pierced his eyes, making the headache throb even more.

"Fuck!" He threw his hand over his eyes, and cursed again when he hit his bruised eye. He really hated pain.

Then he felt something across his chest. Cautiously opening his good eye, Justin looked down and saw it was an arm. His eyes following the length of it, he was surprised to see it belonged to Beth.

And she was sound asleep beside him.

She was gorgeous. She'd always been pretty, but now she was gorgeous. She resembled her mother a great deal, but not just because she had the same blond hair Cassie had, but her body was becoming just as curvy.

The question was, why was she lying beside him in bed, her am draped over his chest?

Rolling onto his side, careful of his bruises, Justin watched her sleep. They'd been friends forever it seemed, yet in the six years since he'd left Passion behind, he hadn't once tried to get in contact with her.

He'd wanted to, God knew he did. But when he'd learned she'd gone off to the city to train to be a cop, he decided not to. She'd always looked up to his father, and now she was a cop, just like him. Justin felt betrayed because Beth knew how much Justin hated his father being a cop.

So he left her in his past like everyone else he had known.

Now he was back, and she was lying beside him, looking as if she was as content as a cat in its owner's lap.

He couldn't help but reach out and touch her soft golden hair.

When her eyes opened, she looked like she'd been caught with her hand in the cookie jar.

"Morning."

She sat up, those blue eyes opening wide. "What time is it?" She spun to the left to look at the clock. "Shit. Why didn't my watch go off?"

"I said, good morning?" When he sat up, the room began to turn. "Shit." He dropped back down, closing his eyes and willing away the dizziness.

"I should have woken you three hours ago. Damn it! Are you okay?"

Her hand on his face felt like silk. "I am now." He opened his eyes and all he saw was beauty. "Were you always this beautiful?"

She pulled her hand away and climbed off the bed. "I should be going."

"What's your hurry?" This time when he sat up, Justin made sure it was slow.

"I…uh...need to get home."

"Why so suddenly? Shouldn't you stick around to make sure I'm okay?" He didn't want her to leave just yet.

"You'll be fine on your own now." Grabbing her jacket, Beth headed to the door.

"And there's that cold shoulder again. What the hell are you doing, Beth? One minute you're punching me in the face, and the next you're playing all nice, taking care of me. Fill me in, because I'm lost."

"You needed someone to watch over you last night, and I just happened to be there," she justified.

Justin stood carefully and walked to her, trying his best to ignore the thumping inside his head. "My dad was there, and he offered to have me stay at the house, so that's not going to cut it." He wiped a finger beneath her eyes at the faint smudge of mascara that had obviously come off during her sleep. "You missed me," he teased.

She slapped his hand away, a scowl on her face. "I was just being nice."

"You missed me." He just couldn't help himself. He'd always loved teasing her because she always got all flushed and defensive.

"Get bent, Justin." She yanked the door open, then with a snap, closed it in her wake.

A smile on his face, Justin walked to the window and watched her drive off. Then his eyes focused on his car. "Fuck!"

Throwing the door open, he marched to the side of the vehicle and stared down at the flat front tire. Looking towards the back, he saw the rear tire was also flat. "Son-of-a-bitch." Taking a tour around the car, he saw all four tires were not just flat, but had been slashed.

And there was only one person he knew who would do that to his car.

"You are a dead man, Wes."

"Oh, my God!"

Justin spun around to his mother's voice, which hadn't been the smartest thing to do because the air around him began to spin. "Shit." He braced a hand on the car and waited out the dizziness.

"You look like hell, baby. Come on, you need to go inside and lay down."

Because he really did feel like crap, he let his mother lead him to his room.

"Your father told me you'd been in a fight, but I never expected it to be this bad. Here you go, lay down now."

"I think I'll just sit." Leaning against the headboard, Justin took a few deep breaths. "He tell you

I was the innocent party?"

Julia clucked her tongue, sitting beside him on the bed. "Yes. That Wes Donnelly has always been a troublemaker. He's out of jail no more than a month and he's out causing trouble again."

"What do you mean, out of jail?"

"Have you eaten? Do you need me to get you anything? You should stay at home, so I can look after you."

"Mom," Justin interrupted before she could continue. "I'm fine. What did you mean about Wes being in jail?"

"He's been in and out of jail since you left, baby. Breaking and entering, theft, violence, assault. He just got out a month ago and came back home to…well, apparently cause more trouble. He should be in jail now after what he did to you, not out roaming around freely. Are you pressing charges?"

He hadn't thought about it. "I don't know." But he was damn glad he'd left when he had. If he hadn't, well, Justin figured he might have been in as much trouble as Wes. "I need to have my car towed to the garage."

"Why? Oh, baby, you really do look like hell."

"Thanks, Mom, and please stop calling me baby. I'm twenty-four years old now, not ten." He slid from the bed, minding his head and dizziness. "You happen to know the number for the garage?"

"You don't want to take your car to the local garage. Wes works there."

Justin frowned. "Great. So where then?"

"I'll have your father call Rusty in Carson Valley. He'll come pick it up and take care of it for you. But for now, I think you need to rest. Have you eaten breakfast yet?"

"No, I just woke up." Which reminded him he'd woken to a very lovely blonde, who despite her anxiousness to leave, had been very cozy cuddled up beside him all night.

"You should come home."

"Mom." He didn't want to stay at the house. It would only cause more friction between him and his father if he did.

"I only meant for breakfast. I could make you a big stack of pancakes and some bacon. How does that sound?"

Delicious. "I could do breakfast."

"Great. Come on then, I'll drive."

~

Half an hour later, he was sitting at the kitchen table, a stack of pancakes and several slices of bacon on his plate. His mother was the best cook he'd ever known, and she hadn't lost her skill in the years since he'd been gone. "As usual, Mom, fantastic grub."

"Thanks, ba—Justin."

He smiled; glad she was finally ditching the nickname that had always irritated him. When he heard the sounds of footsteps on the stairs, he shifted to see his youngest sister groggily coming towards him. "Morning sleepy head."

Abby's eyes shot open and a smile filled her face. Then just as quickly her face went into complete shock. "Oh, my God. What happened to your face?"

His baby sister had always resembled their mother most. Her hair was a bob of springy orange that framed a delicate, porcelain face. She was tall and skinny and as pretty as a peach. "This is courtesy of Beth," he pointed to his left eye. "And the rest is all Wes Donnelley's doing."

"He's back in town?" She looked to their mother for verification and received a nod. "Bastard."

"Abby," their mother warned.

"Sorry." Then she mouthed it to Justin, making him smile, and curse when the cut on his lip stretched. "I was going to come by and see you today." Bending at the waist, Abby rested her head on his and put her arm around his shoulders. "Welcome home, bro."

"Thanks, sis." They'd seen each other a month ago at their grandfather's funeral and both Abby and Donna had been ecstatic at seeing him. And, though he wouldn't admit it to either of them, he'd missed them.

"You save any of those for me?" She fingered his plate of food.

"There's plenty for you, dear," their mother reassured, heaping pancakes and bacon on her daughter's plate.

"So how long you staying, bro?" Abby inquired, taking a seat at the table.

"Not sure yet. I won't be going anywhere until my tires are fixed." His stomach soured just thinking of Wes slicing his wheels.

"What happened to your tires?" Abby asked, pouring enough syrup on her pancakes to make both their and him wince.

The back door opened just as Justin was about to explain it to his sister.

"Just came back from looking at your car," his father stated, pulling his regulation hat from his head to kiss his wife. "Tires have been slashed."

"Yeah, I figured that much out." Lifting his cup of coffee, Justin secretly wished Wes dead. "Two guesses who might have done it."

"Do you have proof?" His father stole a slice of bacon off Abby's plate and received a scowl.

"Hey, get your own. Your tires were slashed?" she inquired of Justin.

"Yeah. No, I don't have proof, but it's not hard to figure out. He was mighty pissed at me last night."

"Without proof I can't do anything about it. In the meantime, I called Rusty and he's heading in to grab your car now."

Justin pushed from the table, his appetite sated thanks to his mother's wonderful cooking. "Then I'll head over there now and meet him. Thanks for the grub, Mom." He kissed her cheek before turning to his sister and ruffling her already messy hair. "Come by the hotel later and we'll catch up."

"You bet."

"I'll drive you," His father offered, kissing his wife once more before leaving. "You feel as bad as you look?"

"Pretty much. So I hear Wes did some time?" He climbed into his father's police cruiser, this time in the front and not as a criminal.

"Yeah, couple of months here and there. Just got out a month ago," his father explained, starting the car and driving off.

"When he came at me yesterday, he was spouting something about me getting away with it. I'm guessing he did some time for the B and E before I left?"

"He didn't do time for that one but was on probation with a hefty fine. He tried it again three months later and that one sent him away for a year. He's been in and out of trouble since."

"And he's pissed at me for that?" Justin snorted. "Wasn't my fault he couldn't keep himself clean."

"I can see him being resentful, though. You got away with it."

Justin's jaw clenched. "I guess nothings changed. You still think I'm guilty."

"I don't think this is the time to discuss it."

"I think this is the perfect time. It's why I came home after all."

"You came home because you promised your grandfather you would. If he hadn't died, you wouldn't be here now." He came to a stop in front of Justin's car. "I'll call if I find out anything about your tires."

"Whatever." Bursting from the car, Justin slammed the door and stomped off to his room. Things hadn't changed. His father still didn't believe him.

~

It was just after three when Justin pulled into his parking space at the hotel. It had taken two hours for his car to be fixed. He was now sporting four new radials, which he wouldn't have needed if the bastard hadn't slashed them. No, he didn't have proof that Wes had done it, but you didn't need to be a rocket scientist to figure it out.

Slipping from the car, he engaged the alarm system, then headed to his room.

"J-man. Hold up."

Justin turned to see a tall, thin, blond-haired young man hurrying towards him. It only took a few moments for him to figure out who it was. The guy hadn't changed much in the years since Justin had been gone. "Kevin?"

"One and the same. Look at you. Holy fuck! Get the number of the truck that ran you over?"

Justin took the hand Kevin held out, grinning. The kid's grip was firm, despite his gaunt frame. He was the youngest of the Healy children and at the tender age of nineteen, had his sights set on an acting career. Or so Justin had been told by his sisters. "Yeah, Wes Donnelly. Good to see you, my man."

"That prick's back in town, I hear. Guess he came gunning for you. Shit. Hurt much?"

"About as much as being barreled down by a truck can hurt. Come into my humble abode and catch me up. Man, you haven't changed much since I saw you last." Justin let them into his suite, tossing his keys on the table. "How's the acting career going?"

Kevin frowned, slipping the sunglasses from his face and propping them on the top of his head. "Slow. I want to go out to Los Angeles and do some bit parts but my parents are being sticklers about letting me go. They say I'm too young to fly off to such a big city and live on my own."

"Well, you are their baby, and I hear it's tough to let the last one go."

"Shit. I'm not stupid, and I can take care of myself. I'll convince them sooner or later. How long you staying in town?"

They settled in the chairs by the table, Justin stretching his long legs out. "Not sure yet. It depends if my dad and I can work things out."

"Wish you luck with that. I hear you're doing

alright for yourself."

"I'm doing better than alright. I own a club called Just in Time and it's one of the top clubs in Mississauga."

"So my parents were telling me. Hey, you should talk to them for me. You made it just fine on your own and you were younger than me when you left."

"It's your biz, my friend. I'm staying out of it." He threw his hands up.

Kevin just frowned. "Why'd you never call or anything? We missed you around here."

"Shit happened between me and my dad before I left, then my mom lit into me shortly after. I guess I was mostly pissed that no one believed me or was on my side." Justin shrugged.

"I never believed for one minute that you helped Wes break into the Gas 'N Gulp. You did some crazy shit back then, but you weren't a thief."

Justin smiled, feeling an ounce of relief that at least one person believed him. "Thanks, man."

"So what are your plans while you're here?"

"Just hanging, I guess." And that thought absolutely bored the shit out of him.

"Wanna grab a six-pack and go surprise Tyler?"

Now they were talking. "You bet."

"It's Friday. He has today off. He's home watching Tommy while Lissy's at work. He'll appreciate the company," Kevin said, getting to his feet.

"Still shocks me that he's married and has a kid."

"That's nothing." Kevin grinned. "Wait until you see him."

Chapter Five

"Holy mother of God!" both Justin and Tyler said in unison.

They stood in the doorway to Tyler's cabin-style house, staring at each other with wide eyes.

"You're huge."

"You're face looks like hell."

Then they both laughed, threw their arms out and grabbed hold for a sturdy hug. "Christ, Ty, you bulked up. You're bigger than your father." He released his old friend, the smile on his face stretching not just his cheeks, but the cut on his lip, also. It didn't matter. What was a little pain anyway when you hadn't seen your best friend in six years?

"I'd heard you'd been in a fight. But damn, Justin." Tyler squeezed Justin's face, making him wince. "Which one did Beth give you?"

"News travels fast. Nothing like small town living." Justin pointed to his left eye. "This one."

"She still has it. Come in. Jesus, it's good to see you."

"Hi, bro," Kevin added with a bit of a sour tone.

"Hey, Kev," Tyler said absently.

"We brought beer," Kevin stated, following the other men into the living room.

"It's still the afternoon. Too early for beer."

Justin sat on a rusty brown sofa that felt like it had been created out of clouds. "Anytime of day is time for a beer. So…shit, I can't get over the size of you. You were all arms and legs when I left."

Tyler sat beside him while Kevin sat in the matching chair across from them. "I got bored when you left and took up weights." Tyler smiled wide, giving his friend a slug on the arm.

"Shit, you must have been really bored. Look at the size of your arms." They had to be at least the same circumference as one of his thighs, Justin thought, and that was just the guy's arms. The rest of his body was big, wide, and muscular.

Tyler grinned proudly, nodding his head. "And you look as puny as ever." He handed him a tissue. "Your lip's bleeding."

"Shit, must have popped a stitch." To remedy it, he pulled out a can of beer from the case and rested it against his lip.

"Wes did a number on you, that's for sure. Guess he wasn't happy to see you were back."

"And then some. He slashed the tires on my car, too."

"Bastard."

"You should see his car, Tyler." Kevin whistled through his teeth. "It is a beauty. Porsche 911."

Tyler's brow lifted, and he swiped his fingers back and forth across his shirt. "Fancy car, my friend. You hit the big time for sure."

Justin shrugged, popping the top of his beer, deciding it was a wasted beer just sitting against his lip. It was just as helpful if he drank it. The alcohol would help sterilize the wound. "Good investments. So I hear you work at the bank giving out loans."

"Loans officer, yep."

"You always loved dealing with numbers. Wasn't my deal, though. And you're married with a kid, no less. How's that working for you?"

"It's great. My wife, Lissy, is fabulous. She's a teacher's assistant at the elementary school. And Tommy, man, he is a wonder. Never thought I would feel so much love before, but my heart swells with it."

Justin let out a burst of laughter, startling Tyler. "Jesus, you sound like that romantic crap they write about in romance novels."

"Ever been in love, my friend?" Tyler asked casually.

"No, and not looking for it anytime soon. You can keep the love, marriage, and kid crap. I'll party enough for the both of us." There was a quick knock on the front door before it swung open. As Justin looked over, Beth waltzed into the house.

"Hey—oh." She stopped short, her eyes focusing on Justin. "What are you doing here?"

"Came by to hang with Ty. What are you doing here?" he asked.

"I...oh, I came by to tell you, Tyler," Her eyes shifted to her brother. "I met Lissy and she said to tell you she'll be late and for you to order pizza for supper. She's helping a few kids do some work after school."

"That's my wife, always lending a hand. You have to stay and meet her, Justin."

"Can't wait. I gotta see the woman that's making my best pal turn to mush," Justin teased, giving Tyler a shove with his fist.

"Great. Hey, why don't you all stay for pizza. It'll be like old times," Tyler suggested.

"Works for me. Dad's making tofu lasagna." Kevin shuddered.

"Beth?" Tyler asked his sister.

"I really—"

"You can feed Tommy when he wakes up," Tyler coaxed.

Beth's face slowly filled with a smile. "Okay."

"She's a softy when it comes to my boy." Tyler beamed, then reached into the case for three beers, tossing one to Beth and another to Kevin. He cracked his open and held it up. "To old times."

"To better times," Justin amended; his eyes still on Beth. He just couldn't get the feeling of her lying beside him out of his mind.

~

The pizza was hot and spicy, the beer was cold, and the conversation was constant. He had friends back home, but not like these. Nothing was better than old friends who knew you the best.

Sitting in Tyler's living room, beer and pizza a plenty, Justin savored the moments.

"Remember that time you guys put a fake snake on my mom's lounger on the patio?" Kevin asked with a laugh.

"Who could forget," Justin chuckled. "I think they heard her screams in the city."

"You didn't get the aftermath like I did." Tyler pulled out another beer. "Man, was she pissed when she realized it was fake."

"I told you not to hang around in the kitchen. You should have run like we did." Oh, those were the good old days, Justin thought.

"What is the point of pulling a prank if you can't be there to see it happen?"

"We had a bird's-eye view from my garage," Justin informed him. But Tyler hadn't listened to them and had stayed in the kitchen, watching his mother from the window. It was even funnier to watch his mother charge after him with the snake, screaming her head off at him.

"Why do guys always think it's funny to make women scream?" Beth wanted to know, turning to Lissy.

"It's the superior manly thing," Lissy explained. "They like to believe they're in control, that they're stronger."

Beth just snorted.

"We are stronger," Justin added, cracking open another beer.

"Right, and who was it who needed someone to hold his hand while the doctor stitched up his lip? You weren't so strong then, were you, Justin?" Beth reminded him.

He narrowed his eyes. "I didn't need you to hold my hand. The doc told you to come in and sit with me. There was no hand holding."

Beth rolled her pretty blue eyes. "He only asked me to sit with you because you went white the instant he said you needed stitches."

"I hate needles," Justin admitted to his pals, who in return gave an understanding nod.

"Aw, the big strong man hates needles." Beth continued to tease.

"At least I'm not afraid of moths." *Take that, Beth.*

Her eyes narrowed, and he could have sworn her face went just a little pale. "I'm not afraid of them. I just don't like them."

"Oh, please forgive my blunder." The sarcasm saturated Justin's words.

"Man, this is just like old times," Tyler sighed, leaning his arm over his wife's shoulders. "I missed this."

So did I. Though they had all grown since they'd last sat around shooting the breeze, so much about them was still the same. Tyler still bit his nails when he was nervous and had done so the instant his wife had come home and introduced herself to Justin. Kevin always flipped his hair back like some fashion god. His hair had always been his pride and joy. And Beth. What could he say about Beth? She'd changed the most out of all of them. Oh, she still liked to give him a hard time, and she still had a sly sense of humor, but she'd changed in other ways. Her hair was a long, golden wave of sunny silk. The stick-figure body she'd had six years earlier was now curvy, full-figured, and incredibly sexy. And she'd become a cop.

He was still trying to come to terms with that fact. Though, seeing her in that blue uniform was an incredible sight. And since she'd stayed with him during the night to make sure he didn't lapse into a coma from his head injury, she'd been mostly civil to him.

"Tommy's awake," Lissy announced when a squawk was heard over the baby monitor.

"I'll get him." Beth jumped up and ran for the stairs.

"She really hates being an aunt," Tyler joked, then glanced up, his face lighting as Beth came into the room with his son. "And here is my boy. Justin, meet my son."

He really had no use for infants. They cried too much, pooped all the time, and when they weren't filling their diapers, they were burping up some god-awful stench that even the strongest stomach churned at.

But when he looked up and saw Beth coming towards him with that baby in her arms, something clicked inside his chest.

"Tommy, meet Daddy's friend, Justin."

Justin tore his eyes from Beth long enough to glance down at the kid in her arms. "Hey. Cute kid." Though he really hadn't looked at it long enough to determine if that statement was true or not.

Beth looked so right, holding that baby in her arms.

"Did you check if he was wet or dirty?" Lissy asked, touching her son's cheek.

"He doesn't smell dirty," Beth cooed against the baby's face.

"But he could be wet. I'll go change him. Come on, Beth, you can help."

"She loves being an aunt but hates changing the diapers," Tyler said humorously.

"Who can blame her," Kevin added with a wrinkle of his nose.

Yeah, Justin pretty much agreed.

For the rest of the evening, he couldn't help but stare at Beth. He couldn't understand it, but for some reason she looked...different to him now.

~

It was well after midnight when Justin staggered from Tyler's house, Beth and Kevin right behind him.

"You're not driving," Beth ordered the instant they stepped out into the cool night air.

"Um…yes I am." His pockets seemed to be smaller than usual. Justin fumbled, trying to get the keys out.

"You've been drinking."

"I'll drive," Kevin slurred, staggering a little.

Beth grabbed his arm to keep him in place. "I don't think so, little bro. I'll drive."

"It's only six blocks from here," Justin justified, finally pulling his keys from the pocket of his leather jacket.

"A lot can happen in six blocks, and as an officer of the law in this town, I can't let you get behind that wheel in your condition." She held her hand out to him, her face determined. "Keys."

Justin's brow curled up at her demand. "I don't think so. I'm fine, Beth. I only had four beers, and I ate enough pizza to soak up all that alcohol. I can drive."

"He can drive," Kevin slurred.

"Now, *he* is hammered." Justin laughed, giving Kevin's hair a rub,

"Not the hair, man. Jeessusss." Kevin stroked it back into place while teetering to the side.

"Give me your keys, Justin, and I'll drive you both home."

"Use your own car."

"I didn't bring it. I walked here."

"Well, you're not driving my car."

"Then neither are you." She lunged for his keys only to have him jerk them out of her reach. "Give me your keys, Justin."

"No," He stepped back when she came at him.

"I'll just lie down in the car," Kevin informed them, wobbling his way to Justin's car.

"Do not puke in my car, Kevin." And because he was momentarily distracted, Beth was able to grab his hand that held the keys. "Damn it!" But when he tried to pull his hand away, their faces collided and sent a blinding white light of pain shooting from his nose right up into his sinuses. Stars flashed before his eyes.

And he lost the keys.

"Son-of-a-bitch, that hurts." He clutched a hand over his throbbing nose; the pain even made his eyes water.

"You shouldn't get into barroom brawls, then," Beth stated, walking to the drivers side of Justin's car, keys jingling in her hand.

"You're the one who popped me in the nose, remember?" Damn, it was sore. "You're not driving my car, Beth." No one but him drove his baby. Well, okay, so he'd allowed his father to drive it, but only because he had been seeing double at he time.

She slid into the driver's side, ignoring him, and turned over the ignition. "Either get in or walk."

Snarling and holding his sore nose, Justin was left with no other choice. Grumbling under his breath, he slid into the passenger's side—had he ever been in the passenger's side of his own car?—then shut the door carefully.

"Seatbelt."

"It's six blocks, Beth."

"Seatbelt," she said again with more emphasis.

Growling, Justin did up his seat belt with a sharp snap. "Happy?"

"Very." She put the car in reverse and backed up.

"I think I'm going to be sick," Kevin slurred from the backseat.

"Stop, stop." Before Beth had come to a complete halt, Justin threw his door open, then went to the back door. With one hand, he pulled Kevin outside and just in time. The kid puked up all the pizza and booze he'd consumed, and then some. "Feel better?"

"Not really." Kevin swiped the back of his hand over his mouth, lifting his head. "But I don't think I'll puke again."

"You'd better not in my car." Opening up the back door, Justin shoved Kevin inside, then slid in beside him. "Start driving."

Ten minutes later, after getting Kevin into the house and into his bed, Beth drove Justin back to his hotel. Even though he'd insisted he could drive the four blocks, Beth still insisted. Well, she shoved the keys in the pocket of her skin-tight jeans, leaving him no choice but to accept.

"Now how are you going to get home?" he asked when she came to a stop at the hotel.

"Walk." She climbed from the car, strolling to Justin to hand off the keys.

"Which is stupid. If you had just let me drive the four blocks, you could have stayed home." He took the keys she held out to him, touching her hand in the process. It was soft like silk.

"I wouldn't be a very responsible officer of the law if I had let you. I like to walk," she justified.

"Suit yourself. You wanna come in for a nightcap?"

"You've had enough to drink. Get some sleep, Justin."

He watched her walk off into the night and was mesmerized by her swagger. He thought how she reminded him of a white knight riding off into the night. Except, she wasn't a knight, and she wasn't on a horse. Maybe he had drunk too much.

Chapter Six

At five in the morning, he'd been awoken to the sound of a car door slamming, what sounded like a bottle breaking, and plenty of cursing. He hadn't thought much about it, figuring someone had had a bit too much to drink and had dropped their booze of choice upon exiting their car. He'd gone back to sleep, forgetting completely about it.

Justin wished he hadn't.

After taking his time in the shower, shaving, and dressing, Justin sauntered from his room, ready for breakfast. His plans were halted abruptly by the graffiti slashed across the hood of his car in blood red spray paint. Every foul word in the book was scrawled on his car, and as Justin stared down at it, his anger grew as red as the paint.

"Fucking Wes." He was a dead man.

Climbing into his car, Justin started it, then threw it into reverse, spitting up gravel when he backed out of the lot. He didn't know where Wes lived, but he knew where the guy worked. Coming to a screeching halt in front of the local garage, Justin slammed out of his car and headed inside.

He was beyond furious.

"Where is he?"

"I beg your pardon?" the young woman at the front desk asked.

"Wes Donnelly. I want to see him. Now!" Justin

demanded, his hands resting on the counter. He wasn't leaving until he pounded the life out of Wes.

"Um…I'll go get him."

Justin paced the floor while he waited for Wes to come out. The bastard was not going to get away with this. First, he'd gotten a shit kicking from the guy, then his tires had been slashed, and now, the vandalism. Enough was enough.

"What the hell do you want?"

Justin spun around, the anger he felt boiling inside of him ready to explode. "You fucker!" He lunged at Wes, only to have the woman step in front of him. "Back off, honey."

"Don't call me honey," she snarled at him.

"I was going to be nice and not press charges against you for beating the crap out of me. Even when you slashed my tires, but now, now there is no way I'm letting you get away with spraying graffiti on my car. You'll pay for this, Wes," Justin threatened, looking around the brunette that stood between them.

"What the hell are you talking about? I never slashed your tires or vandalized your car." Wes snapped back.

"The hell you didn't. You'll pay, you bastard. If not by the law, then by me." Justin meant the threat he just dealt out.

"Is that a threat?"

"You bet your ass it is." He watched Wes pick up the telephone on the counter and dial. "Who the hell are you calling?"

"The cops. Yes," Wes spoke into the phone. "I need a few officers at McCray's Garage, and preferably not a Davis or Healy. I've got a man here making death threats towards me."

"You god damn liar." He lunged again only this time the woman held her hand up palm up, and slammed it into his nose. Justin buckled, the pain slashing deep into his skull. *Fuck, why the nose*?

He dropped to his knees, his eyes watering and his

nose throbbing.

"They're on their way," Wes added, setting the phone down. "Good shot, Dee."

"Thanks. Self-defense classes actually paid off."

Through the blinding pain, Justin heard them babbling. And he heard the car when it approached and guessed it was the cops.

Here we go again.

"What seems to be the problem?"

Holding his nose, Justin looked up to see the very same officer that had been at the bar two days ago. The very officer that had seemed to have a distain for Wes.

Maybe things were looking up.

"This guy came in here, threatening us," Dee explained. "I had to take him down to stop him."

"I came in here to confront that bastard. He vandalized my car," Justin snarled, still holding his nose. He could feel the blood seeping out.

"I never vandalized nothing." Wes shot back, his face contorted, his brown eyes narrowing.

Wes never had been an articulate speaker. "He's full of shit."

"Do you have proof that he vandalized your car?" Constable Millar asked.

Damn it. "No, but—"

"Then you ain't got nothing," Wes spat at him, snorting in through his nose, then spitting it out on the floor.

Jesus, why had he ever hung with this guy? "Fine. I don't have proof, yet. But I'll get it," Justin vowed.

"We got things wrapped up here then?" Constable Millar asked.

"Providing he stays away from me."

"Same goes," Justin spat at Wes. Damn, his nose was killing him. He threw the door open and marched to his car. Moments later, Constable Millar stepped out and called his name. Justin turned, still a boiling pot of anger. "What?"

"What makes you think he did this to you car?" He

pointed his index finger at the graffiti.

"He's pissed at me for something in our past and this is his way of telling me so."

"The incident six years ago, when Wes was caught inside the Gas 'N Gulp? Beth told me you were suspected of being involved."

The guy was not helping Justin's anger any. "I wasn't involved. And Beth has a big fucking mouth."

"Watch what you say about her," Constable Millar warned evenly.

Justin's brow rose. "You two an item?"

"Used to be, not any longer. Look, why don't I look into this..." He jabbed his finger at the hood again. "See if anyone saw anything.

Justin shrugged one shoulder. "Go for it. I doubt my father's done any looking."

"You two have a...tense relationship. I noticed that when he came down after you'd been brought if from the bar fight."

"Yeah, it's strained. Look, I appreciate you looking into this. Let me know if you find out anything." Justin walked to his car, fuming when he caught sight of the graffiti. It was a nice fucking car and now it was soiled with this trash.

"My brother does bodywork out of his garage at his house. Extra cash. Why don't I send him over to have a look at your car?"

"He any good?"

Millar smiled. "The best."

"Sure, send him by." What harm could it do? At least he wouldn't have to take it someplace else and end up using a rental car.

Or maybe he should just get the hell out of Dodge.

Damn promises.

Justin hopped into his car and drove, thinking. The one thing that had given him moments of regret was the argument with his mother six years ago. And the disappointment in her eyes had haunted him in his sleep for weeks after. Because of what she'd said to him, because of that disappointing look in her eyes, Justin had pushed himself harder, worked harder to be a better person. In that aspect, his mother really was the catalyst for his success now.

For the first week after his mother had left him with the ultimatum, Justin had sulked in the room his grandparents had given him. He'd been pissed at his father for not believing him, and yes, angry at his mother for not taking his side. But in the years since, he understood why.

His grandparents had been kind enough to give him a week before his grandfather had set him in his place. His Grandpa Leo was normally a quiet man, but when he had something to say, you could guarantee you would be sitting and listening for hours. Justin figured it was because he'd been a professor and used to lecturing for hours at a time.

So Justin had sat on his bed and listened while his grandfather spoke.

"*You only have one life, Justin. Don't waste it by sulking. You've had your fun, now it's time to grow up and become a man. No more handouts, no more sympathy, no more coddling. You have a good, solid brain, use it for good. Now, get your butt out there and find a job. If you don't have some sort of job in one month's time, I will enlist you in the army and load you on the next bus out of here.*"

He'd said it with such candor that Justin knew he meant it. Justin had hauled ass the very next day and went out on a job hunt. Two weeks later he was working as a busboy at a family diner, making minimum wage. When his grandfather had informed Justin that he would be paying rent, he'd been pissed. But he'd kept his mouth shut and obliged. It hadn't been much, two hundred out of every pay check, but Justin knew that he was getting off easy. He surely wouldn't be paying so little if he moved out on his own. And besides, he always had food in his belly and clean clothes in his closet, thanks to his doting grandmother.

After living with his grandparents for a year, Justin came to realize the inconvenience of living with two elderly people. He never really had any privacy, and they frowned upon him having women overnight. So he'd set out to find a decent yet affordable apartment. His very first home had been a tiny bachelor suite where the only room that had a door was the bathroom. His bedroom was the living room, and he slept on the pull-out couch, which was pretty convenient when you had a woman staying over. All you had to do was seduce her on the sofa; she was already in your bed.

He'd lived there for six months when his grandfather had shown up at his door with an envelope. Justin had invited him in, confused about what he had in his hand. Until Grandpa Leo explained. The two hundred dollars a paycheck that Justin had thought had been for rent had actually been invested by his grandfather.

Justin could still remember what he felt when he looked down at the statement his grandfather had given him, and the amount he'd seen. Fifty thousand dollars, and it was all in his name.

Holy shit!

But like everything that came from his grandfather, there was a stipulation. That money had to be used for something lucrative. Either he used it to go to school and get a degree, buy a house, or something of equal value. Or…he could continue to pay into it for another year and watch his money grow.

If Justin wanted to remove funds from the account, he needed his grandfather's signature to do so. But to put more money into it was of his own accord. He'd been tempted to withdraw it and buy a kick-ass car, but he was sure that wasn't what his grandfather meant by something lucrative. So in the end, Justin decided to keep putting money into the account. At first it wasn't much, he only could spare so much from each paycheck. But then he found another job that paid better.

Two years later he had enough money to buy his own club and enough left over to keep him afloat for the first year.

So, not only did he have his mother to thank for making him want more for himself, he had his grandfather to thank for getting him there.

Pulling into the slot designated for him at the hotel, Justin knew what he had to do.

He had to stick around and make things right.

With both his parents.

~

With his arms loaded down with bags of food, Justin walked up the steps to his parent's front door and rang the bell. When his sister Donna answered, he was totally shocked.

"So, it is true. The prodigal son returns." She stretched up to look into the bags he had in his arms. "With food."

"And you won't get any if you aren't nice to me."

She smiled at him, putting him at ease. "I'm always nice. See," she took one of the bags from him, "I'm helping you with this burden in your arms."

"If it had been cleaning supplies, you wouldn't have been so eager to help. So when did you get in, sis?" Donna was a mix and match of their parents. She had the red hair like their mother, but it was darker, leaning more to the brown side of red. Her eyes were as blue as their father's and she also had his smile, but the rest of her features were the same as their mother's. She wasn't overly tall, barely coming to his chin, and she sported more of a curvy figure than his youngest sister did. And Donna had a wicked sense of humor.

"Late last night. I have a break from classes for the next week, so I thought I would come home and irritate my big brother," she gave him a wicked grin.

"Lucky me."

"Your face looks like hell."

"Doesn't feel that great either."

"Want me to go punch Wes out for you?" she teased her big brother.

His eyes narrowed but he smiled anyway. "Would you?"

She laughed, walking through the house. "What's with all the food?"

They set their bags on the kitchen counter side by side, then Justin began unpacking them. "I thought we'd have a family barbeque."

"You do know it's April, right?"

"It's always barbeque season. Where is everyone?"

"Abby's at work, she'll be done by six. Mom went to help Mrs. Anderson wash her windows, and Dad's still at work," Donna explained, helping herself to a glass of juice.

"Perfect, they'll get home to the pungent scent of fresh meat being barbequed. You make the salad and potatoes."

Her eyes narrowed in on him. "It might be nice to be asked."

"You always run the chance of being rejected if you ask. It's better to order," he remarked with a wide smile.

"Is that how you treat your employees?"

He slung his arm over her shoulder and, with a cocky smile, replied. "Nope, I like my employees."

"Jerk."

His breath rushed out in a whoosh when she slugged him in the gut.

Chapter Seven

Being back home wasn't all bad. Sure he'd had his...mishaps, and sure he was bruised and achy from those...mishaps, and sure his car had gone through a lot of crap, but right now, right here, Justin was happy.

The barbeque had been a huge success. His parents had been surprised, not only to find him cooking in their home, but with the fact that he *could* cook. The steaks he'd chosen had been thick and of the finest cut. The beer was plentiful and ice cold, and Donna had done a superb job with the baked potatoes and salad and she'd even toasted French bread.

They sat around the table like they had so many times in the past, only this time, Justin didn't feel the stress, the tension, the animosity that had so often swirled like tepid steam in the air around them. With their bellies full, everyone sat like stuffed pigs, unable to move. It was a good feeling to know he'd brought his family some long overdue happiness where he was concerned. God knew he'd given them enough sadness.

"We need to have a game of basketball."

Everyone's heads turned to Abby, eyes set in a get-real look. She couldn't possible be serious. Groans were heard around the table.

"Come on." She stood up, placing her hands on her hips. "It's a gorgeous evening, the snow's melted and the ground is dry. It's a perfect night for basketball."

Justin's response was to throw the crust of his

leftover French bread at his sister's face. "Not."

Her face sunk in a sulk of epic proportions. "You're being a party pooper."

"Don't make me hurt you, Abby," Justin warned.

"I'll pin her and you can tie her up," Donna offered.

"That involves moving." And there was no way he could even string together enough effort to think to move.

"Well, these dishes aren't going to clean themselves." Pushing from the table with a groan, his mother began clearing the dishes. "Who's helping?"

"Basketball sounds like a blast." With a sudden burst of energy, Justin jumped from his chair.

"I haven't whooped your ass in a long time, bro." Donna stood, slugging her brother on the shoulder.

"Dream on, squirt." Planting his palm on her face, Justin gave her a shove.

"Let's snag Kevin and make it a foursome," Abby suggested, heading for the back door.

"Guys against girls," Justin called out, pushing past his sisters to get to the back door.

"They don't have a hope in hell." Donna got a nod from Abby, then high fives were exchanged.

"You gals keep dreaming. I'll go snag Kev." Feeling pretty damn good, Justin sauntered over to the Healys' and knocked on the back door. When Beth answered, he felt his day getting even better. Her hair was pulled up in a bouncy tail of gold. She wore a baggy blue t-shirt and blue jeans and didn't have a stitch of make-up on her face. She reminded him of the young girl he'd once known. "Hey."

"Hey yourself."

He had no idea why, but he was suddenly speechless.

One finely tapered golden eyebrow arched when Beth spoke. "You're here…why?"

"Oh, oh, right. I came to see if Kevin wanted to play some basketball with Donna, Abby, and myself."

"He's out on a hot date."

"Oh, well, what about you? Feel like getting hot and sweaty and beating my sisters in a few games?" She seemed to hesitate in thought, and Justin was ready to beg. *Beg? Where the hell had that come from?*

"Why not. I could use the exercise."

Casting his eyes from her head all the way down the length of her body, Justin couldn't see why. She had to be the fittest women he'd seen in a long time. The muscles in her arms were slightly defined and didn't look frail and puny as they had in her youth. Her chest—well, that definitely had shape and plenty of it. Her waist was thin and gave way to a curvy set of hips that led to a pair of very long legs. God, what he would love to do to that body.

Holy hell! Was he lusting after his best friend?

"Are you just going to stand there or are you going to let me pass?"

"What?" Sweet God, his mouth was dry and his heart was pounding and he was pretty sure he was about to get a hard-on.

Stop thinking about her, damn it!

"Do you want to play with me or what?"

"What?" Had she just…

"Jesus, Justin, what is with you? Move." With a shoulder check, she nudged him aside and walked through the door.

It took him a few moments to gather himself before he finally stepped outside. When he was hit with a gust of cold air, he gave silent thanks to the gods. It was enough to shock him out of his lustful thoughts.

He could only hope the wind carried him through the game.

~

"You did that on purpose."

"What?" Julia asked while she gathered up the dishes left on the table.

"You knew the instant you mentioned dishes, they'd scurry out of here like rats running from a hungry cat."

"I don't know what you're talking about."

Vic stood, taking his wife's hands in his to stop her. "You know perfectly well what I'm talking about. Now, you either did that to get them out of the house so we had some free time," he wiggled his eyebrows at her, "or you wanted to talk about our son."

"The first one is tempting, but it's the second one."

"Damn, a guy can hope."

Julia gave him a shove then began gathering dishes. "You get plenty of sex."

"Plenty, yes, but there's always room for more."

"Behave. So..."

Deflated, Vic lit a cigarette and leaned back in his seat. "What?"

"What do you think?"

"About what?"

She set the dishes in the dishwasher, shifting her glance to her husband. "About Justin."

"What about him?" He wasn't sure he wanted to have this conversation. Yet.

"He seems to be genuinely trying to make amends."

He blew out another stream of smoke over his head, watching it dissipated in the air. "If you say so."

Letting out a long sigh, Julia leaned her hip against the cupboard. "You don't think so?"

Vic shrugged, tapping his cigarette out, then stood to help his wife. "Why'd it take him this long? Sure, we knew where he lived, we knew how he was doing, but he never called home, not even once a year to wish us a Merry Christmas. Every time one of us called him, he never called back and when we went to see him, he was never around. Now, because his grandfather dies, he suddenly comes home because he made a promise. I can't help but feel it's a vain attempt to clear his conscience because of the promise." He shook his head. He hadn't wanted to open this can of worms. "I need some air."

Leaving his wife to clean up, Vic headed out the

front door.

~

They were tied, Abby and Donna on one team, Justin and Beth on the other. His sisters had definitely been practicing while he'd been gone. Abby was all arms and she'd smacked him more than a few times in the jaw with her elbows. Donna was sneaky and maneuvered around him with lightning speed. He was taller than both of them, and Beth matched his height, but the two girls were definitely giving them a run for their money.

"What's the matter, grandpa, you need a break? You're looking a little pale, and you're huffing like a steam engine," Abby taunted him, getting right in his face while he dribbled the ball.

He narrowed his eyes and with his free hand, slapped his palm on her face while he pivoted around her. Taking the shot, he jumped up and slammed the ball right into the basket. "Take that! Now who's huffing and puffing? And look at the sulky lip." He poked her bottom lip and pulled his finger away when she chomped her teeth together.

The air rushed out of his lungs from the sharp elbow to his rib cage, which of course, caused him to drop the ball. Donna scooped it up with a laugh.

"You're losing it, bro. How quickly they forget."

"I haven't forgotten anything." He remembered quite well how his sisters used to double team him. While one distracted him, the other one would take in her shot. Rubbing his ribs, he wasn't sure if he was glad that some things hadn't changed with his sisters.

"Are we going to finish this or what?" Beth piped in, bouncing on the balls of her feet, her stance very much like that of boxer.

God, she was magnificent.

"Loser buys ice cream," Donna chimed in, tossing the ball back to her brother.

Half an hour later, Justin leaned against the garage, catching his breath. His sisters had given him a good run, and in the end, they reigned victoriously.

Damn them.

"I think I'll have a triple scoop of mocha fudge." Abby squished Justin's cheeks together with her hands while she taunted him.

He slapped her hand away, snarling. "What do you think, I'm made of money?"

"Well, yeah," she said with a wide toothy grin.

He smiled now, giving her a shove. "Well you're right. Okay, let's get the baby her ice cream cone. You coming, Beth?" Again she hesitated and again Justin felt the nagging urgency to beg her.

"Sure. Mocha fudge sounds great."

"I'll drive." They headed to the front where Justin had parked his car, all three women stopping to look at the graffiti on the hood. "I'm getting someone to look at fixing that tomorrow."

"He's a bastard," Abby scoffed.

"You don't know who did it," Beth piped in.

Justin brow curled. "I know perfectly well who did it, I just don't have the proof."

"Who do you think did it?" Donna inquired, climbing into the back seat.

"Wes Donnelly," Abby added, climbing in beside her.

"Pure conjecture," Beth continued justifying.

"Jesus, you even sound like a cop." Justin started the car moving along.

"Um, maybe because I am a cop. That's a stop sign."

"I know it's a damn stop sign." And to make the emphasis that he was going to stop, he came to a sharp halt, sending everyone lurching forward in their seats. "Happy?"

Her blue eyes narrowed at him and he felt his heart trip just a little bit more.

"Not particularly. If I hadn't been in the car, would you have stopped?"

He pulled up at the local Dairy Delight, swiveling in his seat to face Beth. "Of course I would have." When she snorted at him, rolling those pretty blue eyes he suddenly had the strongest urge to grab her by the neck and plant a hot one on her lips.

"Are we going to get ice cream or argue?" Abby broke in, poking her head between the two of them.

Justin pulled out his wallet, yanked a twenty out and handed it to his sister. "Go crazy." He wasn't done with Beth yet. The instant his sisters left the car, he engaged the locks, jailing Beth in the car with him. "What was that snort about?"

"Nothing. Unlock the door, Justin."

"Not until you tell me what the snort was for." She simply stared at him, so he gave back just as much. Several moments of staring passed, neither breaking down. Justin was stubborn, and he knew Beth was equally so.

"Want anything?" Donna asked, knocking on Justin's window.

"No!"

"I'd like—"

"Nothing until you answer my question," he cut Beth off with more than his words.

"Oh, for pity sake, Justin. Fine, the snort was because I didn't believe you. What's the big deal?"

"The big deal is that you didn't believe me." She threw her hands up and shook her head so he forged on. "It pisses me off that no one believes me. Believes *in* me," he added.

"Well, honestly, Justin, what do you expect?"

"I expect an ounce of trust from people I love and have known all my life."

"All this because I didn't believe you were going to stop at the stop sign?"

"No, not just because of the stop sign. Damn it!" He threw his door open and began walking off his anger. When he heard her door close, he didn't bother to turn around but knew that she was following him. "I buy expensive steaks, get all the makings together for a superb dinner for my family, and surprise them with a barbequed meal when they get home, and still I sense an air of disapproval from my old man. Sure, he smiles, he jokes, he looks like he's having a good time, but I see it in his eyes."

He continued to walk, kicking rocks in his path as he took angry steps. "What the hell's it going to take for him to trust me?"

"Trust has to be earned, Justin."

He stopped short, turning to Beth. "What the hell does that mean?"

"Well, if you want to be trusted, you have to—"

"I know what the statement means, Beth. I meant what do you mean by it?" She let out a breath, then pulled the band from her hair and gave it a shake. Justin nearly lost the breath in his lungs watching all that gold tumbled down around her face.

"You think that by buying expensive steaks and making a meal, your parents are going to just brush the past away and forget what you did?"

"I didn't do anything," he said with gritted teeth. She snorted again and it only made him angrier.

"Do you honestly believe that? Come on, Justin."

"What?" She was really pushing him.

"You want me to go down the list of shit you pulled in your youth?"

He crossed his arms over his chest and glared at her. "No, I don't think I'd like that."

"Of course not, because denial is your middle name." She turned away only to have him grab her by the arm and yank her back.

"You're not leaving until we finish this."

"Everything okay over there?" Donna called out.

"Yes."

"No," Justin snarled at Beth.

"We are finished. You don't want to hear what I have to say therefore we're done. Let go of my arm."

He released his hold of her but stood right in her face telling her clearly he wasn't letting her go until they were done. "Fine, just say it, Beth."

"You were a troublemaker in your youth. You enjoyed pissing your father off, you enjoyed making him sweat, and you didn't give a damn about his job and how often *you* put it in jeopardy."

"You make me sound so callous."

She shrugged, holding out her hands.

He couldn't believe what he was hearing. "Fuck you." Shoving his hands in his leather jacket pockets, he stomped off. He didn't need this shit anyway.

"That's right, walk away. It's what you do best."

He spun around and saw her jump back at what had obviously been the furious look on his face. He certainly was feeling furious. "Don't push me, Beth."

"To hell with it. You need someone to tell you like it is and if you want to deck me after, well, then we're even."

"I don't hit women."

"Fine, good. Do you have any idea how much you hurt your family, your friends by running off and not calling, not writing?"

"I was pissed at them for pushing me away."

"Because you tried to pit them against each other. Yes, I know about that. I overheard our parents talking when your mom got back. She was devastated, she hated having to push you away, but it was the only thing she knew to do. You hurt her and your father deeply when you did that."

"I had no choice. My father didn't believe me when I said I wasn't involved with Wes when he broke into the store. He took Wes' word over mine. His own damn son!"

"Oh, so pitting them against each other was payback. My God, Justin." She shook her head, then continued. "And why should he believe you? Every time you and Wes got together, you were in trouble."

"Now you're just exaggerating." And he wasn't enjoying this conversation one bit.

"Not by much. Look, all I'm saying is that if you want respect and trust from your parents, you need to give it time. Everyone just needs some time to get used to you being back and get over the Justin we used to know."

"Does that include you?"

She hesitated before replying. "Yes."

"So that's what the cold shoulder's been about."

"We were so close, best friends, Justin, and you leave, no word, no calls, for six years." She emphasized the last, then walked away, sniffling.

Was she crying? Oh, shit, she was. "Beth—"

"Don't." She continued walking, her head down and Justin felt his heart crack.

"She has a point."

Justin turned to see both his sisters standing before him like two walls. The look in their eyes said it all. "Not you, too?"

"We love you Justin, but..." Abby began.

"It hurt when you never called," Donna finished.

He felt like he was being ganged up on and just wasn't prepared to deal with it. "I think I need some time to think." Pulling the keys from his jacket pocket, he tossed then at Donna, then walked away. "Park it in my stall at the hotel."

Chapter Eight

She should be feeling relief now that she'd cleared her conscience. Yet Beth had tossed and turned all night long after leaving Justin. Maybe she'd been too hard with him; maybe she shouldn't have told him how she felt about his leaving. But damn it, he'd pushed her into spilling her guts. And telling him the truth might actually knock some sense into that thick head of his.

Yet she still felt bad for going at him the way she had.

"Penny for your thoughts."

Beth looked up to her mother's smiling face shining down on her, and it brightened her mood just a little. "'Morning."

"It has been for me for quite some time already. You look perplexed. What's up?" her mother asked, walking to the cupboard, pulling out a cup to fill it with coffee.

"I was just thinking about Justin."

"There's news. When aren't you thinking about Justin?"

It was true, she thought about him a lot, though she wasn't too sure she liked the fact that her thoughts were so transparent. "We had a fight."

"Again, there's news." With her cup in hand, her mother sat at the table. "What was it you fought about this time?"

She and Justin had been best friends since they were

infants, and yes, they tended to argue, both being very opinionated. But their fight last night had been more hurtful. She hadn't meant it to be that way, yet.... "I told him the truth about how I feel about him."

Cassie's blue eyes lit with glee. "You told him you're in love with him?"

"No!" Beth gasped, looking around to make sure no one had overheard. The last thing she needed was for her gossipy younger brother to know how she felt about Justin. "I told him how much his leaving and not calling for all this time hurt me."

"Okay, so how did that end up in the two of you fighting?"

Beth lifted the cup of coffee she'd poured when she'd come down for breakfast, and when it touched her lips, she realized she'd been sitting at the table for a good long time. Her coffee had gone cold. "It all started with him nearly running a stop sign and my disapproving. It sort of snowballed from there, ending in me blurting out what a louse he was for leaving and never calling. You should have seen his face, Mom. He was so hurt."

"Hmmm, might be good for him, though."

"I know, that's what I was thinking, too, still..."

"Everyone's a little touchy when it comes to Justin, and rightfully so. I love the kid to pieces, but part of me thinks of him as a coward, running away and hiding the way he did."

"I know," Beth sighed, dropping her head. "I feel the same way."

"It'll take time for everyone to get over the animosity we feel towards him, especially Vic and Julia." Beth looked up when her mother's hand laid over hers. "And you. But it's not going to be easy."

"Yeah." It certainly wasn't easy. And she was trying desperately to forgive him, yet...

"He'll sulk for a bit, like he always does, then he'll come back as usual and act like nothing happened." She squeezed Beth's hand as she stood. "But it's up to you to decide if you want to let him. Put something in your system besides the coffee."

Beth sat at the table a long time after her mother left, knowing what she said was true. Justin would sulk, then he'd suck it up and ignore everything she'd said to him. Only this time, Beth decided, she wasn't going to let him.

~

Justin pulled into the warehouse-style garage and came to a stop just where Dillon Millar instructed him. He hadn't expected such a professional looking garage, but it looked like this guy knew his business and knew it well. The grey coveralls he wore were smeared with grease indicating his profession.

Justin climbed from the driver's side of his car, closing the door softly before walking to Dillon. "So how long do you think this will take?"

"A few hours to prime and paint, then a few more after that to dry. You come back...say, eight this evening, and she should be good. Mighty fine car, shame what was done to it."

Justin couldn't agree more. "Here's my cell number. If you have any problems or need to ask me something, it's always on." He handed Dillon his business card with his cell number on it.

"You own a bar, huh?" Dillon asked, looking down at the card.

"Yep."

"Do much business?" He tucked the card into his greasy pocket.

"A fair amount." Was he fishing to find out if Justin had enough money to pay him for the work that would done on the car?

"Wish we had a better bar here. That damn country crap they play is enough to make a man gag. Give me some good old fashion hard rock and I'm a happy camper."

"You and me both, dude." When Justin saw Constable Millar enter the garage, in plain clothes, it surprised him more than a little. Then he remembered the two were brothers.

"Hey, Mark. How's it going?"

"Not bad. Are you going to be able to fix her up like she was?" Mark asked, nudging his head to Justin's car.

Dillon snorted. "Damn straight."

"Figured as much. You have a minute, Justin?"

When Mark crooked his head indicating he wanted Justin to follow him outside, he nodded. "Call me if you have any problems," he called back to Dillon.

"She's in good hands, my man. Don't worry," Dillon responded, walking to the car.

He hoped so. That car was his pride and joy. His baby. "What's up?" he asked when he'd closed the garage door.

"I've been asking around, kinda casual like, just to see if anyone knew anything about your car."

Mark had Justin's attention now. "Yeah, and…?"

"Couple people say they overheard Wes having a good old time over your misfortune. Saying whoever did it should get a medal of honor."

Justin's hands curled at his sides.

"But he isn't admitting to having done it, or the tires."

"Figures."

"So there isn't much we can do about it without proof."

"And let me guess, no one saw anything either."

Mark shook his head, somberly. "Sorry."

"Yeah, no one more than me." Justin tucked his hands in his jacket pockets. "What do you have against him?"

Mark kicked a clump of dirt on the ground, his head down. "Who said I have a grudge against him?"

"I just got that impression the other day in the garage when Wes called in on me. What did he do to you?"

Mark let out a long breath before responding. "He

dated my sister two years ago. Got her pregnant, then told her to deal with it herself. Dumped her the day she told him. She lost the baby a week later."

"I'm sorry."

"Yeah, me, too. I didn't like her dating him to begin with, but, well....sisters."

Justin chortled. "Tell me about it. I have two."

"You have my pity, brother. I try hard not to show my dislike for Wes, but, hell...sometimes I just can't bottle it. You know?"

"Oh, I know." He knew all too well. Even thinking about Wes got his temper up. "So, now what?"

Mark shrugged his large shoulders. "I keep an eye on him; keep asking around and hope the bastard slips up at some point."

Justin wasn't going to hold his breath. "Thanks, Constable."

"Call me Mark. Take it easy, Justin."

"Thanks. You, too." It was nice to actually have someone on his side.

~

There was a crispness in the air, but the sun baking down definitely alluded to the summer warmth that was just around the corner. May was approaching and trees were beginning to bud. Even the tulips and irises were starting to break their way through the chilly ground, in search of the warm sun.

Beth enjoyed the sunny day while she meandered down the streets. It had been Vic's policy to have his officers stroll about the town, rather than ride through it in their vehicles. His thought was that it was more personal to have them walking around than in a car. They could interact with the townsfolk easier on foot and people became more comfortable with them. And Beth also enjoyed it.

She stopped here and there, to talk to someone strolling along the street or interact with children playing in their yards. Plenty of people were taking advantage of the warm weather and were out working on their gardens. She caught up on the gossip around town and was never disappointed with the jokes that were so often told. Everyone knew her by name but respected her rank.

When she saw Justin sauntering down the street, her heart skipped a beat. Damn, he was nice on the eyes, always had been, and he had such a sexy swagger. That dark leather jacket he wore made him look even more menacing. He was the embodiment of a bad boy, and it made her body ache for his touch. Always had, even in his pimple-faced teenage years. She couldn't remember when exactly she'd realized that she was in love with Justin. Maybe she'd always been in love with him.

His hands were in the pockets of that gorgeous leather jacket he wore. His jeans fit snugly to long legs and a nice, firm ass. She'd noticed, *oh, boy*, had she noticed. He'd bulked up some since she'd seen him last. And like always, when those gorgeous blue eyes with those killer long blond lashes lifted to her, she absolutely melted.

"Hey." His lips curved up in a wry smile that tugged at her already pounding heart.

"Hey," she replied, reminding herself to stay calm. She'd been reminding herself to stay calm around him for years. "Where's your car?"

"Dillon Millar's fixing it up. Painting over the graffiti."

Her head bobbed in a nod. "Good. He'll do a fabulous job. How long before it's fixed?"

"He said later today."

"Yeah, he's good, and he's fast." She was suddenly struck dumb for words.

"Just out for a walk?"

"Daily walk about the town." Feeling uneasy, she shifted her feet, tucked her hands in her jacket pockets.

Now Justin's head bobbed in a nod. "My dad still has his people doing that, huh?"

"Everyday. It's a good policy." She felt so awkward with him, not just because she was so damn madly in love with him, but because the last conversation they'd had didn't end up that great.

"Sure. So, what time are you off?"

She loved when he ran his hands through his hair, like he was now. She'd imagined doing so for more years than she could remember. "Seven."

"Feel like doing something?"

Oh, God, yes. She shrugged. "I don't know. I'm usually pretty beat after work."

"Then maybe we could watch a movie."

She wanted nothing more. "Maybe another time." It was killing her to say no, but she knew it was what she had to do. He was doing the very same thing he always did after an argument that didn't go his way. He pretended it never happened. Well, enough was enough. This time, he had to realize he was to blame and he needed to deal with it. "Why don't you call Kevin or Tyler?"

His face deflated. "They're both busy. Kevin has a hot date with someone he referred to as Ever-Ready Betty." He shook his head.

"He's still young and thinks life revolves around sex."

Justin snorted a laugh, nodding. "Sweetie, life does revolve around sex."

She hoped to God she wasn't as red as she felt. "Well, I should get back to work."

"I'm sorry."

She stopped short but didn't turn back to him. "For what?" She waited with bated breath.

"For being an ass yesterday."

She actually felt her insides quiver. But did he really mean it? Looking at him, she could see the sincerity in his eyes. "Only yesterday?"

He smiled, the left side of his mouth lifting just a smidge higher than the right. "Funny. I'll let you get back to work."

Beth watched him turn away and walk down the street. He really did have a damn fine ass. She waited until he was nearly across the street when she called out, "I still like horror movies."

He stopped, looking back, that crooked smile bowing just a bit higher. "Scream fest it is. I'll have the popcorn ready when you get off of work."

Smiling to herself, she continued on her walk.

~

Thank God the local video rental place had the latest releases. Standing before the shelves of movies, Justin had no idea what Beth had seen. She still liked scary movies, but there weren't that many out. *Saw III* was one, then there was *The Ring II*, and three others he wasn't sure she would be interested in. Maybe it was best to go with *Saw III*. It had blood, terror, suspense, and a good dose of gore.

Perfect.

"I thought you would've left town by now."

Justin's shoulders bunched at the sound of Wes' voice beside him. He didn't bother to give the guy his attention and slipped the movie from the shelf.

"How's the car?"

His fingers tightened on the cover he held in his hand. The bastard had some nerve. And the fact that his car was taking longer to fix than expected only made him hate Wes more. Still ignoring him, Justin walked to the front desk and paid for the movie. All he needed was to stop for some microwavable popcorn, some beer or coolers, and he was set for the evening. Stepping outside, Justin saw Wes leaning against the building, smoking casually. If he went in the opposite direction he knew Wes would know he was trying to avoid him.

So he did the only thing he could and walked past him.

"Going to watch a movie with mommy and daddy?"

Justin continued to ignore him, even when Wes started following him. It was only three blocks to the convenience store, he could handle it.

"On foot. Not using the car? Embarrassed by the

graffiti or the truth that was written on it?"

Two more blocks.

Wes quickened his steps until he was right beside Justin. "You really are a bastard, you know that."

"Fuck off, Wes." Damn it, he shouldn't have spoken.

"You waltz into town with your shiny new car, dressed in designer clothing, but we all know the truth about who you really are."

When Wes jumped in front of him, Justin bunched his fists, ready for the fight.

"Trash."

His jaw clenched, but Justin refused to indulge Wes.

"What's the matter, pretty boy? Cat got your tongue?" Wes prodded on, walking backwards in front of Justin. "Who'd you have to blow to get all this money you've been flashing around?"

Justin pivoted, trying his best not to let Wes get to him. But it didn't seem to matter which way he went, Wes was right there, in his face.

"Was it your granddaddy? I heard you went to him when your daddy kicked you out. Bet it was your granddaddy. Bet you enjoyed it, too. Did you, Justin? You enjoy blowing Granddaddy for money?"

Justin's fist curled, and he would have been more than happy to smash the bastard's nose in, but the smug look in Wes's eyes was what stopped him. He lowered his fist and went for the verbal punch instead. "You'd know all about blowing someone to get what you want, wouldn't you, Wes? How was prison, by the way?"

For a split second, Justin thought he was going to be in for another round of fist to the face. Then Wes, spun around and marched off.

Justin watched Wes walk away. Though he'd been victorious, he certainly didn't feel good about it.

Chapter Nine

Rushing from her house, Beth darted to her car and once inside, shoved the keys in the ignition and pulled away from the curb. She took a second to glance at herself in the mirror and was relatively happy with what she saw. She'd rushed home from work, changed out of her uniform and into a pair of jeans and a button-down shirt. There hadn't been much time to fix her make-up; thankfully it was still intact.

It was stupid to be feeling excited about spending the evening with Justin. Yet she was. Her insides were jittery, her belly tight, and her chest ached. She told her self to relax, but it did little good.

She'd run the gamut of thoughts after seeing Justin. Was she doing the right thing? Maybe she shouldn't be spending time with him yet. He was only going to hurt her again if she opened herself up to him.

But in the end she'd pushed all thoughts aside, deciding to just spend the evening with an old friend, and what came of it, came of it.

As she pulled up to the hotel, her stomach tightened just a bit more.

Taking a deep breath, she slipped from the car, then, after another breath, walked to his door. When he opened it, smiling at her, all thoughts floated away.

"Sorry I'm late." Did she sound as breathless as she felt?

"No real time was set, so technically, you're not. I

got *Saw III*; I hope you haven't seen it yet?"

"Nope, not yet."

"Great. I'll start the popcorn; help yourself to a beer or a cooler. I got both."

She pulled out a vodka cooler and popped the top while Justin put the popcorn in the microwave. She'd never been in the local hotel, which seemed a little odd, given her profession. Yet the calls involving incidences in the hotel had never come on her shift. It was a decent looking place, she supposed. It looked clean, smelt clean, so that was a plus.

"I realized when I got back here that watching a movie on this pathetic excuse of a TV was kinda pointless. We might both suffer eye strain."

She laughed, feeling a little uneasy now that she was here, alone, with Justin, in his hotel room. "I guess I should have brought my binoculars."

"Wouldn't have hurt. Popcorn's ready."

It smelt like heaven. Pulling up a chair beside the bed, Beth made herself comfortable.

"What are you doing?'

"Sitting?"

"Over there, in that uncomfortable chair?" He sat on the bed, placing the bowl beside him then patted the vacant spot. "This works better."

Beth hesitated before climbing onto the bed with him. She'd slept beside him not long ago, she could handle sitting beside him to watch a movie.

She hoped.

"Do you remember that time our parents went to the city for dinner and we rented one of the *Friday the 13th* movies and Abby peed herself with fright?" Justin laughed as he brought the beer to his lips.

"I remember I was pissed off at you when I found out you'd stolen it from the video store."

He set the beer down with sneer. "I borrowed it."

"Without paying for it."

"Semantics. I gave it back."

"And you think that justifies it?"

"Are you going to play Madam Justice every time I bring up something from my past?"

His voice had a clip to it she knew very well. He was annoyed with her, and though she hadn't mean to, she'd upset him when he was only trying to reminisce. Still… "Not every time," she joked with a faint curve of her lips.

He stared at her with narrowed blue eyes before responding. "I paid for this movie, if you're curious."

"I wasn't. It's a tad harder to steal movies these days. All the movies are behind the counter rather than in the cases." His eyes narrowed just a bit more and she realized what she'd said and how insulting it had seemed. "What I meant was—"

"You still think I'm capable of theft. I've changed, Beth, though none of you care to see that."

"Maybe because we haven't seen you for six years." What was she doing? She didn't want to get into a fight with him. "Look, I wasn't trying to be—"

"A bitch?" he finished, cutting her off.

She bit her cheek, her temper rising. "I knew this was a bad idea." She slid off the bed, setting her cooler on the bedside table.

"Where are you going?"

"Home."

He jumped off the bed, putting his beer on his bedside table. "I'm sorry I called you a bitch. Look, I'm a little touchy tonight. Wes was in the video store while I was there and he followed me, taunting me. I shouldn't let him get to me, yet…"

"He followed you?" Her cop instincts kicked in.

"On foot. Give me a second chance here, Beth." He held his hand out to the bed.

She couldn't help but wonder if the word he chose was meant for more than just tonight. Though she knew she should just leave, she found herself walking back to the bed and sitting down.

"Thank you." He took his seat, grabbing the TV remote.

"If he continues to bother you, let me know."

"I can take care of myself." He started the movie and the advertisements began.

"Says the man with the bruised and battered face."

"I took care of myself just fine. Sure, I came out the worse for wear, but he knows what I'm capable of."

"Sure, capable of passing out like a girl." She smiled at him, hoping to alleviate the tension.

"You looking to take me on, Healy? Because I can show you here and now what I can do."

She was sure he could, and that thought alone stirred enough juices inside of her to make her uncomfortable. "I know what you can do, Justin." She sat up, then placed her left hand on her forehead and swooned, "I feel faint," then fell back, faking blacking out. It was hard not to burst into laughter.

"That's it. You are going down, Healy."

Jumping up, Justin straddled her and her heart began galloping beneath her chest. Then he grabbed her sides. She lost her breath while he tickled her mercilessly, writhing about trying to get him to stop. "I can't breathe."

"Now who's the pansy? Come on, tough cop. Is that all you've got?"

Her ribs were beginning to ache with laughter and if he didn't have her arms pinned down with his legs, she could fight him off easier. In a surprise move, he captured her mouth in a sharp possessive type of kiss that took her breath away.

Beth wanted nothing more than to give in to the pleasure of the moment and let the kiss sweep her away. But she didn't want to be a casual fling for Justin while he was home for however long he decided to stay. Lifting her knees up, she twisted her body and threw him onto the bed. She sat up, took a deep breath and told herself not to think about how warm and inviting his mouth had been.

"I came to watch a movie, Justin, nothing more."

He sat up and that soft sexy look he had in his eyes

nearly melted her reserve.

"Are you absolutely sure about that?"

"Positively." *Hold it together, girl.*

Letting out a long breath, Justin shrugged then leaned back against the headboard. "Then a movie it is."

With regret swirling around inside of her like an F5 tornado, Beth leaned back and gave her attention to the TV. Thank God there was enough gore in it to take her mind off of sex. Taking a handful of popcorn, she watched the movie unfold.

"What are you doing?" she asked moments later when she felt Justin's hand in her hair.

"Playing with your hair."

"Well, stop it."

"Why? You used to like it?"

She still did, and that was the problem. "Not any more." She shifted just a skosh further away and grabbed her cooler. He lowered his hand and Beth felt both relief and regret.

Sliding further down on the bed, she watched the movie, her eyelids beginning to droop.

~

Justin heard the thin rasp of breath and, looking over, saw that Beth was fast asleep. God, she was pretty. He face was so soft, not a blemish marring the beauty. She had a cute little button nose and thick full lips. They'd practically melted to his when he'd kissed her. He'd love to kiss her again. Forgetting about the movie, he rolled onto his side and watched her sleep. All that golden hair of hers fell onto her shoulders and unable to resist, he ran his fingers along the silk. She moaned, indicating she enjoyed what he was doing and he smiled. *Liar, you still like having your hair played with.*

She rolled onto her side and her hair fell over her face. With a cautious finger, he slipped it behind her shoulder then not being able to resist, ran his hand down her arm. When she smiled, he closed his eyes and froze the moment in his mind.

~

Her body felt the chill and, wanting to be warm, she snuggled into the bed and the warmth pressed into her back. Something was draped around her waist and she tried to pull it closer to ward off the chill. When she hugged it to her chest, it grabbed her breast and her eyes shot wide open.

It was a hand.

Alarmed, she shoved his arm aside and sat up. And in doing so, she saw by the dim light through the window that the sun was beginning to rise. She'd spent the night in Justin's bed.

"Come back here."

Looking over at him had been a bad idea. He looked so sexy, so alluring with his eyes barely open, half asleep. "I have to go." She jumped out of the bed, fighting the urge to do just as he asked.

"Why? It's barely morning," Justin slurred, sitting up.

"Precisely why." Grabbing her jacket, making sure her keys were in the pocket, she pulled the door open, ready to leave. She slammed the door on his protest and ran to her car, checking to make sure no one had seen her. She pulled out of the lot, her heart pounding from the revelation of what she'd done. She'd spent the night with Justin. Oh sure, she had once before when he'd had the concussion, but this was different. She'd gone to his hotel to watch a movie and had ended up falling asleep. And had woken in his arms.

Pulling up to the curb in front of her parents' home, Beth hurried to the front door and slipped the keys into the lock. She stepped into the house, quietly, and was tiptoeing her way to the stairs when her father spoke up.

Scaring the living breath right from her lungs.

"Good morning."

She halted in her spot, and after taking a quick breath, walked to the kitchen where her father sat at the table. It was barely five in the morning. Why was he up? "You're up early." Earlier than usual.

"I have a plane to catch at ten."

"Ahh." She began to slink down the hall and when he cleared his throat, Beth paused. Taking a deep breath, she turned around. He crooked his finger in his direction and Beth walked into the kitchen. *Here it comes.*

"Did you enjoy the movie with Justin?"

She wanted to crawl into a hole and die. "Very much." Not that she could remember what had happened after the first hour. "I know what this looks like, Dad, but it isn't what it looks like. I fell asleep."

Her father held his hand up to stop her, then spoke in that deep slow way he had. "What you did or didn't do is none of my business. You're a grown woman. Just remember who you did or didn't do anything with."

"I don't think I understand what you're saying." And since she was up, she poured herself a cup of the coffee that was already brewed and waiting.

"I just don't want you to get hurt. I love Justin with all my heart and I truly think of him as family, but I know what he's capable of. I don't want him hurting my little girl."

"As you pointed out, Dad, I'm a grown woman, but I appreciate the concern. I know what Justin is capable of and that's exactly why I'm not letting him get to me." *Well, mostly.*

"I'd wished so desperately that you would find someone while he was gone and forget your affection for him. But it looks like that hasn't happened. You love him, baby, don't you?"

"I really don't want to get into this." Not that she didn't feel comfortable talking about it with her father; she was always comfortable talking to him about anything. Her emotions were just too raw right now to discuss it. She walked to his side and leaning down, kissed his cheek. "Have a safe flight and a good art show."

"Thank you. I'll only be gone two days, but you can always call me on my cell if you need to talk."

Smiling, Beth leaned her cheek on his head—she'd always loved the feel of his long silky hair—and replied, "I love you, Daddy."

"Love you, too, baby girl."

She walked up the stairs to her room and grabbed what she needed for her shower. While the water ran, she stepped beneath the stream and let the tears flow.

Why did love have to hurt so damn much?

Chapter Ten

Fresh from the shower and feeling somewhat alive, Justin headed out. These early mornings were going to kill him. He was used to sleeping until three in the afternoon, but was also used to working until four in the morning at his club. He wasn't there every night, but at least five out of the seven. And since his condo was above the bar, he could come and go as he pleased.

But since coming back to Passion, he'd been waking before seven. He really needed to black out the window in his hotel room so the damn sun didn't blind him at first light.

This morning, however, he hadn't minded the early wake up. What guy didn't mind waking up beside a gorgeous blonde asleep in his bed? If only that gorgeous blonde hadn't run out the place like it had been on fire. He was having a great deal of trouble trying to figure Beth out. One minute she was spitting fire at him, the next watching a movie with him. She seemed to want to spend time with him, yet she had a habit of bringing up his past more than he cared for.

Okay, so he'd been a bad ass, and yes, he'd been in his fair share of trouble, but that was the past. This was now. Why couldn't she—everyone—get over it?

"I know you."

If the little old woman hadn't stepped in front of him, he would have kept going. "Probably." It was a small town, everyone knew everyone.

"You're the chief's boy. Jason."

"Justin," he corrected.

"Right. You were always in trouble. Boy, did you give him a tough time."

He wished now that he'd just maneuvered around her and kept going. What the hell was he supposed to say to that?

"You've grown some, got some looks on you, too. You're a bit old for pulling any crap now, so keep that in mind."

He smiled brightly while inside his temper flared. "Yes, ma'am." He didn't bother to catch her name before walking off, though she looked vaguely familiar. It was bad enough that his family and friends were throwing his past in his face, now strangers on the street were doing it, too.

Fucking dandy.

"Justin Davis?"

Looking back, Justin recognized the tall, thin man as his grade twelve teacher. "Mr. Harris?"

"You haven't changed much. Oh, you've grown, but you still look the same. I'd heard you were back in town."

Justin nodded, sliding his hands in the pockets of his leather jacket. "Came home for a visit. How have you been?"

"Still teaching at the high school. How about you?"

Something in the guy's voice said, "Still in trouble?"

"I'm doing great. I own a bar in Mississauga that's allowing me to live quite comfortably."

"No kidding. Good for you. I always knew someday you'd get your life together. All you needed was to stop hanging with no good Wes. Well, you take care now. It was nice seeing you again."

"Same here." He went in one direction and Mr. Harris in the other. The guy was right; Justin's life had changed when he'd stopped hanging with Wes.

Because he'd been told to let himself into the

garage, and that his car would be waiting for him, Justin headed around to the back of Dillon Millar's property and opened the garage.

There she was; there was his baby. And lord did she look good. Gone was the bright read graffiti, back was the luscious black. Oh, how he'd missed his car. The guy did wonderful work.

The keys were in the ignition—which didn't sit well with him—anyone could have come in and stolen it. Then again, this was small town no where. Lifting the envelope on his seat, he walked to the large automatic doors and pressed the button. The instant he was behind the wheel and the car was started, he tore open the envelope and read:

Justin,

Sorry I couldn't have it ready last night. The paint took a little longer to dry then I expected. Hope you're satisfied with the job.

P.S.

It damn near killed me not being able to take that girl out on the highway for a test run.

Take care,

Dillon

Smiling, Justin laid the note on the seat beside him, and pulled out of the garage. After running back and closing the door, he headed off. Everyone loved his car.

~

Stepping up the front steps, Justin could smell the heavenly aroma through the screen door. He tapped his fist against the door once before opening it. "Something smells heavenly." He found his mother in the kitchen, her hands caked in flower and a table full of pies and other tempting pastries. On the stove something was bubbling in a huge pot and all the scents mixing together make his stomach growl. "What is all this?"

"Don and Lisa Roberts are celebrating their fiftieth

wedding anniversary and I'm catering it. Don't touch," she barked at him when he reached out to sample a brownie.

He sulked, then walked to the pot. "You still do that? What's this in the pot?"

"Yes I still cater, and that is stewed chicken. Don't touch," she said again, and again he sulked.

"Can't I at least taste something?" It was cruel to have all this food before him and he wasn't allowed to touch any of it.

With her lips pursed, his mother opened the cupboard, pulled out the bag of cookies and handed it over to Justin. "Here."

Was she serious? "You want me to eat some stale cookies made in a manufacturing plant by cold steel when I could be savoring homemade delicacies made with a loving hand?" He clucked his tongue, hoping the guilt would award him plenty of treats.

"Sucks to be you, doesn't it," she laughed, setting the bag on the counter.

"A loving mother would allow her only son at least one tasty treat."

"Not going to work, baby. I'm used to your antics by now. Tell you what. You help me finish these pies and I'll give you one to take home with you."

She was a conniving one. But he supposed it wasn't so bad, considering the rewards. "Okay, what do you want me to do?"

"Bribery always works." She held her cheek out to him to be kissed.

He obliged her and tasted flour on her skin. It reminded him of his childhood and warmed his heart.

"You can scoop the strawberries and sauce into the pie when I place it in the pans."

When she continued rolling out the crust, he dipped his fingers into the bright red sauce and sampled. It was sweet yet tangy and tempted him to want to taste more.

"Don't touch the food before you wash your

hands."

Frowning, he walked to the sink and scrubbed his hands down. The woman had eyes at the back of her head. "How long have you been at this?"

"Since dawn."

"Aren't you sick of doing it yet?" He scooped in the strawberries, then the sauce into the shell she'd handed him.

"Never. I love cooking and baking."

"You sound like Grandma. She says the same thing." His grandmother had owned a bakery up until four years ago when she'd sold it and retired. But she'd told Justin several times while he'd been living with her and his grandfather that she missed baking daily.

"I learned everything I know from my mother."

"And you both are phenomenal at it. It's a wonder we aren't all fat."

"If you choose your ingredients properly, using low fat oils and butter, along with sugar substitutes, they aren't as unhealthy. Add a little more sauce to the crust."

He poured another spoonful onto the strawberries, then watched her cover it and pinched the edges tight. "You need your own place."

"I have my own place."

"No, I mean your own shop, restaurant, bakery, something."

"I'm just fine here."

No, she wasn't. She should have her own place, where she could cook whenever she wanted whatever she wanted and everyone in town could come and enjoy what she'd made.

And he was going to see to it that she did.

"I heard you got your car fixed up."

He shook his head clear of his thoughts. "Yeah. Dillon Millar did a phenomenal job."

"He usually does. Any word on who did it?"

"I know who did it." He added strawberries and sauce to the next pan she held out to him. He actually enjoyed this, working beside his mother. "There's just no proof."

"Maybe he's gotten it out of his system and he'll leave you alone now."

Justin snorted. Like that was happening.

"You don't think so?"

"I know so."

She turned to him. "Why? What else has he done?"

"It's nothing. So, when is this shindig happening?" he asked, filling another pie, hoping to change the subject.

"Saturday. Is Wes still bothering you?"

"He's trying to, but I'm not letting him. I'm not going to be here much longer; I can deal with him while I am."

His mother stopped rolling the dough to look at him. "You're leaving so soon?"

"I've been here a week." He snagged a strawberry and was surprised when his mother didn't slap his hand.

"Oh," she sighed.

"Did you think I was going to stay longer?"

She shrugged, then went back to her pies. "It's been nice having you home again."

Aside from the face beating he'd received on his first night home, the vandalism to his car, and dealing with Wes, it hadn't been so bad being home again. But he had no intentions of staying forever. A week was long enough. "I have to get back and check out my bar. I left while they were renovating and I have to make sure it's going as planned." The bar was scheduled to re-open in three weeks.

"Right."

The sadness in her voice sunk right to his heart. "I'll be back, Mom."

"Sure,"

She didn't sound convinced. And he supposed he couldn't blame her. "I promise. And you, Dad, Abby, and Donna can come see me sometime."

"Of course."

She still didn't believe him. And he knew just what to do to convince her that he wasn't going to be an absentee son again.

~

It was odd to see his friend sitting behind a desk. Yet there was Tyler Healy, looking all business like in his brown suit and red tie, tapping away on the computer before him. And like old times, he was coming to his friend to ask for money.

In their youth, Justin had often borrowed money from Tyler for a case of beer or take a girl out for the night or simply gas money. It occurred to him now that he owed his friend a great deal.

Clearing his throat, Justin got his attention, and when Tyler looked up at him with a wide welcoming smile, Justin thought how much the man had changed. "I was told to come on in. So, here I am."

"Good to see you again. Face is looking better. Have a seat."

Justin took the metal framed chair with cushions in tweed and went straight for it. "I'm here to ask for a loan."

Leaning back in his chair, Tyler let out a bold laugh. "My, how familiar is this."

"Yeah, I was thinking the same thing. I probably owe you a couple hundred by now."

"Closer to five, I'd say, but who's counting. So, what kind of loan are you looking for?"

Was it really that much? Hell. "A business loan. I want to start a restaurant for my mom."

Tyler's brown eyes lit wide. "No kidding. Where?"

"Here."

"Here? In Passion? The place you hate?"

"It's for my mom," Justin clarified.

"Still, I imagine you'll have to be here while it's being built, to hire staff and to make sure it's running well. Which also means you'll have to be here longer."

Justin pursed his lips. Tyler was right, he would have to do all of that which did mean he would have to spend more time in Passion. But it wasn't like he was moving home for good. "Only until it gets off the ground. I can be back home and still oversee certain things."

"Sure. Why'd you decide to start a restaurant for you mom?" Tyler asked, pulling out his keyboard and beginning to type

"She deserves it."

"For putting up with you all those years, hell yeah. But why else?"

"She deserves it because she is a phenomenal cook."

"Can't argue with you there. She made this gorgeous three-tier cake for our wedding that was to die for. You should have seen the detail she put into it." He shook his head, whistling through his teeth. "It truly was something."

"Hence the reason I want to do this for her. She doesn't know what I'm planning though, so mum's the word."

Tyler nodded and kept typing. "Okay, so let's get this ball rolling then."

~

An hour later, Justin had the loan in the works and was ready to get started. He was excited about the restaurant and couldn't wait to get started. There was a lot of work that needed to be done, but he wasn't daunted by it. In the end, it would all be worth it just to see the smile on his mother's face.

As he headed to his car, he saw Beth standing beside it, dressed in her uniform looking so damn sexy. He had the most incredible urge to grab her around the waist and nuzzle the skin beneath her ears. But when he came up beside her, he saw the ticket book in her hand. "What are you doing?"

"Writing you a ticket."

"I can see that. Why?"

"The meter ran out." She snapped the ticket off and handed it to him.

He didn't bother to glance down at it but kept his eyes on her. "You're joking, right?"

"I never joke where my job is concerned. You can pay that at town hall."

"I know where to pay the damn thing. Come on, Beth," he held the ticket out to her, "give me a break. I was busy with Tyler. I put an hour in but the meeting ran a little long.

"Then you should have run out here and plugged the meter."

"I was with your brother," he emphasized.

One golden lined eyebrow arched arrogantly. "And…"

"He's family."

"I've given my family tickets, also."

His mouth dropped open. "You're kidding me, right?"

"As I said, I never—"

"Kid where your job is concerned." He finished for her. "I know. Damn woman." She was a hard nut to crack. But he reluctantly tucked the ticket into his jacket pocket. "Were you late for work this morning?" Did her face just turn red?

"No." Turing away from him, she began walking down the sidewalk.

It *had* been red. She'd been blushing. Why was she blushing? "Wait up, Beth."

"I'm busy, working."

"You can talk while you're working. Did you want to do it again tonight?"

"I'm busy."

She smelled good, but he couldn't place the fragrance. "Oh. What about tomorrow?"

"We'll see."

"I'll call you tomorrow, then." She waved him off, walking away and Justin stood there just a little longer, drawing in her scent.

Chapter Eleven

He hadn't been in the bar since the incident with Wes. Nothing had changed; they still played that twangy country crap. Spotting Tyler and Kevin in a booth towards the back—like he could miss Tyler's huge hand in the air waving at him—Justin headed through the crowd.

"Place is hoping," he said, sliding into a seat beside Tyler. "So what's shaking, boys?"

"I'm on spring break and enjoying my free time," Kevin stated, then took a sip of his beer.

"Lucky you." Justin looked Tyler over. "The wife unlock the restraints for the night, to let you out?"

"I'm the master of my domain," Tyler boasted and received a chortle from Kevin. "Got something to say, Kev?"

"Nope." Instead he mimicked snapping a whip.

"I am not whipped," Tyler stated with narrowed eyes.

"Sure, bro. Whatever you say." Kevin rolled his eyes at Justin.

"You two are a riot. So, what's shaking?"

"Me, I gotta take a piss." On his feet, Kevin headed to the washroom.

"Kids, they have such a way with words. Do you remember when we used to tie him up in the tree house and leave him there for hours?"

Tyler smiled fondly, then took a sip from his beer.

"Those were the good old days."

"Wanna see how long it'll take him now, to untie himself?"

"Should we let him get drunk first?"

"I'm thinking that might be a good idea."

"It's a deal."

They were both laughing when Kevin returned.

"What's the joke?"

"You," Justin added, then took a sip from his beer to stop his laughter.

"Funny. So, I met this hot chick last week at school," he began and Justin and Tyler looked at each other with knowing glances. "She needed some help in chemistry so I offered to tutor her."

"I bet you did," Tyler snickered.

"Oh, I tutored her alright, if you know what I mean." He winked at them and they both shrugged. "Virgin. She'd never had sex, so I taught her how to do it."

Tyler sighed and Justin leaned back in his seat with his beer. "Want a medal?"

Kevin's brow wrinkled. "No. I just thought I'd share with my pals. Since Tyler here is only getting laid once a week, and Justin has yet to get laid while he's here."

"Unless you're spying in my bedroom, you have no idea how often Lissy and I have sex."

"And what makes you so certain I haven't gotten laid while I've been home?" Justin asked, despite the fact that Kevin was right. He hadn't had sex since he'd been back.

"This is small town life where gossip is the antidote to the addiction."

"Just because I haven't been seen with anyone doesn't mean I haven't had anyone in my room."

"Like Beth," Tyler added casually.

"Yeah, like Beth—wait." He looked back at Tyler. "How did you know Beth was in my room?"

"You had sex with Beth?" Kevin asked with wide

eyes.

"No." He turned back to Tyler and waited.

"Lissy helps clean at Mrs. Henderson's across the street from hotel. She mentioned to Lissy that she saw Beth hightail it out of the hotel at just past five this morning."

"What, does the old woman have a surveillance camera set up to watch the neighborhood?"

"She likes to get up early and watch the sun rise," Tyler explained, finishing off his beer. He signaled for another.

"If you didn't have sex with Beth, why was she leaving you hotel room at five in the morning?" Kevin wanted to know, leaning his elbows on the table, waiting for an answer.

"We were watching a movie and we fell asleep—why the hell am I explaining myself to you? We're both grown-ups, and if we decided to have sex, it's our business."

"She's my sister," Kevin added darkly.

"And…"

"It's fine if you want to bang some anonymous skank, but not my sister."

"Are you saying your sister is a skank?" Justin threw back with a dose of humor.

"You know that's not what I meant."

Justin shrugged. "Look, we didn't have sex and all I'm saying is that if we did, it would be no one's business but our own."

"Do you want to?" Kevin pursued.

"Will you listen to this guy? Yeah, hell yeah. She's hot."

"She's Beth," Tyler added.

Justin lifted his brow. "And…"

"You grew up with her, you were best friends. We don't want her hurt," Tyler informed him.

"And you think I'll hurt her?"

Both brothers shrugged. "We just don't want you thinking of her as a quickie while you're here," Kevin stated.

"I would never do that to Beth. Man, aren't you two the protective brothers. Trust me, I won't hurt Beth. Want another beer, Kevin?"

"Not done this one yet."

"Might as well be prepared." Justin called out to the waitress for more beer and smiled the whole time.

"Okay, what's so funny?"

"Nothing. So, tell us about this virgin you bonked."

~

Kevin Healy had always been gullible, but now that he had a couple beers in him, he was even worse. The dumbass actually believed Justin when he'd asked for rope to secure the car to the post at the hotel so no one would steal it.

Kevin had dutifully gone into the shed for the rope, and all the while, Justin and Tyler were splitting a gut outside, waiting for him.

They sobered up when he came back outside. It wasn't easy, though, when they saw the rope dangling from his hands.

"Here you go, my man," Kevin slurred, holding out the rope to Justin.

"Thanks." God, it was hard not bursting out into laughter. In a swift motion, Justin grabbed Kevin's hands and Tyler grabbed hold of his feet.

"What the fuck?"

"You, my man, are such a fool." Now he could let the laughter free and did so while he wrapped the rope around Kevin's wrists. He handed the rest to Tyler, who made busy work of tying up Kevin's feet.

"Aw, Jesusss guys, come on."

Kevin was plastered, which made this even more fun. He could barely fight with his sluggish arms. "Think we should gag him? It is after eleven." Justin asked, watching the kid flip about like a fish out of water.

"Might not be a bad idea. Give me one of your socks." Tyler held his hand out.

"Why mine?"

"I'm not wearing any." Tyler held up his sockless foot clad in sandals.

"Good point."

"No, wait, not the sock. Come on, guysss, give me a break," Kevin pleaded, trying to roll away from them.

"Think we should give him a break?" Justin asked Tyler.

"If he promises not to start screaming like a girl."

"I won't, I won't scream," Kevin promised.

"Think we can trust him?"

Tyler rubbed his chin, looking down at his little brother. "I don't know. Remember that time he promised he wouldn't tell our parents when he caught us drinking in the bush by the school?"

"That's right. The little fink ratted on us. Nah, we can't trust him." Pulling off his sneaker, Justin began peeling his sock off.

"No, wait, stop. I'll start screaming and wake everyone up and then you'll both be in trouble."

"Everyone *is* already awake," Beth quipped, stepping through the screen door of her parents' place. "What the hell are you three doing now?"

"Tying Kevin up," Tyler replied nonchalantly.

"Why this time?"

"Felt like it. It was long overdue." Tyler shrugged.

"Plus, he was making us sick with his talk of tutoring the virgin," Justin added, then gave Tyler a high five when he threw his hand in the air.

"You gotta help me, sis," Kevin begged, lying on the damp ground.

"We want to see how long it will take him to until himself now. What was his record before, Ty?"

Tyler rubbed his chin in thought. "I believe it was twenty minutes and thirty-five seconds."

"See if you can beat that one, little man," Justin laughed, kneeling down to Kevin.

"He's drunk," Beth stated.

"Yep." Justin smirked as he stood.

"That's a handicap. You should give him at least five minutes to try before starting the watch."

"Good point."

"Beth!" Kevin shouted.

"Gonna help us drag him up to the tree house?" Justin asked her.

"Can't, tree house was torn down a few years ago," Beth informed him.

"What?" Justin looked up at the tree and the vacant spot where the tree house they had all helped build had once been. "Damn."

"Leaving him lay on the ground works, too." Turning, Tyler pulled up a lawn chair and sat.

Following his friend, Justin grabbed two chairs and held one out to Beth. "Ladies first." She took the chair and the three of them sat back and watched Kevin flail about, trying to untie himself.

He couldn't remember the last time he'd had this much fun.

~

"Think we should help him?" Cassie asked, watching out of their bedroom window.

"Nah, Kevin's capable of dealing with this on his own," Thomas added, watching his youngest son squirm about on the ground.

"Just like old times," Cassie sighed a few moments later. Kevin was still squirming about on the ground.

"Yep, it sure is."

~

"Twenty-five minutes and ten seconds. And that's with the five minute head start." Justin laughed, watching Kevin toss the rope aside. "It's true what they say. Drunk people really are slower. Huh?"

"You guys are dead." But just as Kevin lurched at his brother, sister, and Justin, vomit spewed from his mouth.

"Sweet Jesus." Jumping back, Justin barely made it out of the way of the vomit. "Aim it the other way next time.

"Fun's over now." Tom stepped outside. "Come on, son, let's get you to bed. What was his time now?" he asked while he hoisted his son up, tucking his arm around Kevin.

"Twenty-five minutes and ten seconds," Justin recited with a smirk.

"Not your best time, but then again, you had a belly full of beer."

The poor kid really did look green. Justin had only a moment of regret before he let it go. Served Kevin right for boasting about banging a virgin.

"I'd better get going. Lissy's probably wondering where I am."

Not being able to resist, Justin made the whipping sound to his friend.

"Bite me." Shaking his head, Tyler walked off.

"Well, I should get to bed."

Justin looked over at Beth, his heart suddenly speeding up. "It's early, wanna go for a drive?" He didn't want her to leave yet.

"I have to work early tomorrow morning."

"A short drive, then." Where had this sudden desperation to be with her come from?

"Another time." She walked to the door only to have Justin pop up in front of her. "What are you doing?"

"I don't want you to go yet." His heart seemed to be hammering beneath his chest and he had a tightening feeling in his groin that he knew would only get worse until he had her.

"You don't have a choice. Move out of my way, Justin," she warned him.

"I want to kiss you again."

She held up her hand, her eyes narrowed. "I'm not going to ask again. Move out of—"

In a bold move, he yanked her against him, wrapping one arm around her waist while his mouth closed over hers. He felt her straining against him, felt her hand come up and when she planted her palm against his chest to push him away, he held a little firmer. When he finally felt her ease up and her fingers curl into his shirt, he deepened the kiss.

When she jerked away from him suddenly and ran into the house, he stood there staring blankly.

What the hell was with her?

Never one to give up easily, Justin looked up as the light went on in her bedroom. Glancing at the trellis leading up the side of the house, he wondered if it would hold his weigh now, like it had back when he was a teen sneaking up to Tyler's room.

Deciding there was no way of finding out unless he tried, Justin hurried to the trellis and, taking a deep breath, started climbing. Halfway up, he blew out another breath and kept going. The thin wooden rungs creaked here and there when he stepped on them, and by the time he was at the top, and on the roof, he was damn glad the thing held up.

With careful footing, he inched his way to Beth's bedroom. Sliding the window open and slipping in, he was disappointed when he didn't find her in her room. But when her door opened and she entered wearing a very short cotton t-shirt that came barely mid-thigh, he nearly swallowed his tongue.

"What the hell are you doing in here?" She ran for her closet and grabbed a robe.

With great disappointment, he watched her cover herself in the ratty looking terry robe.

"Get out!"

"Not until—" She shushed him and he lowered his voice. "Not until we talk." Or get horizontal in her bed.

"There's nothing to talk about."

He grabbed her wrist when she passed and yanked her towards him. "Okay, then we won't talk." He sunk into her lips with a demanding force and swallowed the moan of protest that came from mouth. She tasted like minty toothpaste and smelled of honeysuckles. Taking her hands in his, he held them against his chest while moving her backwards towards the bed.

When she pushed him away hard enough for him to bump into the wall, he actually growled.

"Stop doing that!"

"Come on, Beth, we both know you wanted me to do that as much as I did."

"You arrogant bastard," she hissed at him.

"Maybe a little, but I know what I feel when we kiss. You want me."

"I do not!"

He shook his head. "You spent the night with me, twice now."

"The first time was only because I wanted to make sure you didn't have a concussion. Last night was because I was beat and couldn't stay awake."

"Great excuses, my dear, but both times I woke up you were plastered against me and that wasn't out of worry or tiredness. You want me."

"Get out." She yanked her bedroom door open, demand in her eyes. "Now."

"Fine, I'll go." He sauntered towards her, but before he left, he leaned in with a quick kiss. "But we aren't finished with this."

He heard the door click shut behind him when he walked towards the stairs.

He smiled all the way home.

Chapter Twelve

The last time he'd been heading out of Passion he hadn't bothered to say goodbye to anyone. This time, however, he felt obligated to do so. He'd already said his goodbyes to his friends and his mother, the only ones left were his father and Beth. Since he knew both she and his father were working today, he figured on killing two birds with one stone.

The office was quiet, like it was on most days. Justin didn't know how anyone could stand working in a place with no activity. He'd be bored out of his mind in less than five minutes.

He walked up to the front desk, sending Millie a brilliant smile. "Morning, gorgeous."

She looked up at him with a smile wide that showed off her brilliantly white false teeth. "And to you. Are you here to see your father?"

"You guessed it. Is he in his office?"

"Yep. Want me to announce you?"

"Nah, I'll surprise him. Hey, I'm heading out of here today. It was nice to see you again, Millie."

"Same here, Justin. Nice to see you've straightened your life out."

He nodded in response, then headed down the hall to his father's office. He had straightened his life out; he just wished more people would see that and forget about his past.

"Knock knock," he said, poking his head inside the

office. His father was on the phone, but he motioned with his hand for Justin to enter.

"I'll be there. Talk to you then." His father hung up and looked up at Justin. "What's up?"

"I'm heading home today. I wanted to come by before I left." Was that disappointment he saw in his father's eyes?

"Oh, well, it was good to see you again."

There was still that distance between them and Justin wondered if it would ever be filled. "Yeah, same here." He pulled out his business card and slid it over to his father. It not only had his work address and phone number, but his cell and his home number. He'd written his home address on the back, which was above his bar. "In case you need to get a hold of me, or…you want to take some time off and visit me."

His father nodded, taking the card from his desk. "We might just do that. Have you let your mother know you're leaving?"

"I told her yesterday that I had to get home. I left while my place was being renovated. I need to get back and check out the progress. I was planning on heading over to say goodbye to her after I left here. Is Beth in today?"

"She is, but she's on the road. Highway patrol," he informed, tucking Justin's card in his breast pocket.

"Oh." He'd really wanted to see her before he left. "Well, I guess I should be heading out." He stood, feeling a tad bit awkward when he held out his hand to his father. "Take care."

His father took it, gave it a sturdy shake. "You, too."

He left his father's office feeling as if he'd just said goodbye to a stranger. He wished to God just once he and his father could get along.

~

Justin found his mother in a near frantic state when he showed up at the house. She was packing food into boxes and checking each one off the list while she went along.

"Getting ready for the anniversary party?"

She nodded in two quick bobs. "Yeah. I'm running late. You can take the next box, Abby," she instructed when Abby entered the back door.

"Hey, sis."

"Bro." Abby grabbed the next box and headed back out.

"I won't keep you long, then. I just came to say goodbye." When his mother's eyes flashed up to him with a wide-eyed look, he swallowed hard.

"You're leaving? Today?"

"Yeah. I need to get back. It was great to see you again, Mom." He opened his arms and she went to him eagerly. She smelt like apples, strawberries, and stew and all those scents would remain with him on his travels home. He had really missed her.

"Oh, I am going to miss you." She clung to him, her arms wrapped tightly around his waist.

With a kiss to the top of her head—something he wouldn't have been able to do six years prior—he released his mother. "I'm going to miss you, too. But I'm not that far away, and I gave Dad my phone numbers and address, so you guys can come visit me sometime. And I'll be back home before you know it." And just like his father, Justin saw the disappointment in his mother's eyes. "I will," he reiterated.

She nodded, sniffling. "I know. You drive carefully now."

"I always do." He kissed her cheek, then turned to the door when his sister walked through. "I have to roll, Abby."

"Like leaving town?" she asked, shocked.

"Yeah. I have to get back to my life. I can't believe how much you've grown, little sis," He took her in his arms and gave her a bear sized hug. "Don't be a stranger. Call me. Dad has my numbers."

"I will. Damn it." She sniffled.

Smiling, he wiped under her eyes with his thumb.

"I'll be back."

She nodded, biting back her tears.

"This is for you."

He saw the box his mother held out to him and when looking inside, he found not just one pie, but four. "Wow. I thought you couldn't spare any?"

"I made a few extra, just for you."

His face lit when he leaned down to kiss her cheek again. "You're the greatest Mom ever."

She sucked back her own tears. "And don't you forget it."

"Never." He looked to his sister, then back to his mother. He couldn't believe how much trouble he was having actually making himself leave. "Well, I'd better go."

"Be safe."

He nodded to his mother, then with feet that felt like they were made of lead, he walked out the door and to his car.

It hadn't been this hard leaving the last time.

~

Justin sat at the junction that led to the highway and away from Passion. He'd been sitting there for nearly five minutes now.

He backed up, ready to turn around, then shook his head and pulled forward. He'd be back, he had to come back. He was building a restaurant for his mother, which was going to need his supervision.

Putting the car in gear, he checked for traffic before pulling out onto the highway. Glancing in his rearview mirror, he watched his home town slowly drifted away behind him.

Damn, he was going to miss everyone.

~

It was end of shift and Beth couldn't be happier. Not that she didn't enjoy her job, she loved it, she was just in a funk today. Justin's late night bedroom call had left her tossing and turning for the better part of the night. Her body had ached for his touch; her mind had told her to forget him. She'd battled the war of emotions the entire night, and had, a few times, picked up the phone to call his hotel.

But each time she'd set the phone down without dialing.

She was a coward, but it was better to be a coward then to have your heart broken, and she was damn sure Justin would end up breaking her heart.

He had before when he'd left without a word.

Pulling her police cruiser into the lot, Beth climbed out, locked the doors after grabbing her clipboard and headed inside the depot.

"Hey, Millie. Any messages for me?"

"Nope. It was a pretty quiet day. What about the highway? Any trouble?"

"A few speeders, one breakdown but nothing out of the ordinary. The chief still here?"

"In his office. Justin was in earlier. They seemed to have a decent visit; at least I never once heard their voices raised."

Beth smirked. "That's a good sign. Catch you later, Millie."

"Have a good night, Beth."

With one quick tap with her knuckles, Beth pushed Vic's door open. "You busy?"

"Just finishing some emails. How was patrol?"

"Dull. I heard Justin came in to see you?" She didn't sit, but she did removed her hat and give her hair a shake. It felt good to let it fall free.

"Yep. Did he get in touch with you before he left?"

Her heart stopped. "Left?"

Vic cocked his head to the side. "He headed back home. You didn't know?"

The pain sliced through her chest with one sharp blow. "No."

"Oh, well, he asked where you were. I told him you were on highway patrol."

She nodded, biting back the pain and the tears that were stinging her eyes. "Well, we never expected him to stick around, did we? I just thought I'd check in before I headed home. Catch you tomorrow."

Beth left the depot with her head held high and her shoulders squared. Even when she climbed in behind the wheel of her car, she kept a stiff upper lip. She drove just past the outskirts of town then pulled into an abandoned lot. Putting the car in park, she sat staring out the windshield. Though the sun was setting, she saw nothing but gray. Her heart was broken, and forever it would remain the same.

He'd left again, without saying goodbye to her. Even after the night before when he'd vowed not to let her go without a fight, he'd left. What had he hoped for, a quickie before heading back to his wonderful life? One quick roll in the hay with an old friend, then back to the floozies she was sure he bedded when he was in his own surroundings. He had some damn nerve.

She lowered her head, resting it on the steering wheel and let the tears flow. They were hot and fierce and ran like a river from her eyes.

How could he have done that to her? How could he be so cold, so callus, so cruel?

And why did she have to be so head over heels in love with the bastard?

The sun slowly began to slide away as she sat in her car and wept.

~

Sitting in his hotel room, Justin pulled out his cell phone and dialed. The drive from Passion to Brandon had been a long one, and even with the heavy beat of rock music blasting out his eardrums, he wasn't consoled. He hated having gone without saying goodbye to Beth. Maybe he should have left a note for her, but that was so impersonal. He'd wanted to hold her in his arms, kiss her one more time before heading out of town. Now all he had was the memory of her lips on his from the night before.

He dialed her home number, hoping to get her before she went to bed. When the phone rang six times without being answered, he hung up. He didn't want to leave a message on the answering machine for her, for anyone else to pick up and listen to. Maybe she was still at work.

With hope, he dialed the police depot and when a male voice answered he figured Millie had gone home for the day. "Can you tell me if Constable Beth Healy is still there?"

"Constable Healy is off for the night. May I ask who is calling?"

"That's fine, I'll call back tomorrow." He hung up, setting the cell phone on his nightstand. Damn, where was she?

Kicking his shoes off, Justin began to disrobe and settle in for the night. He set his alarm for five a.m., wanting to be back on the road as early as possible.

Sliding beneath the covers, his mind drifted to the night before when he'd held Beth in his arms. He remembered quite vividly how she'd felt pressed up against his chest, her bare breasts covered by thin cotton had molded against him. And when she'd drawn in a breath, and exhaled, they'd pressed harder against his chest. He'd felt her nipples grow while he kissed her and he knew she'd wanted it as much as he had.

Why she pushed him away was beyond him.

He closed his eyes, shut out the light and imagined what she would feel like, naked, beneath him, when he penetrated her.

As he drifted off to sleep, his lips curled in a smile.

~

Beth tossed and turned in her sleep, vivid dreams of Justin holding her in his arms, kissing her, caressing her, left her restless. He was so gentle, so loving when he touched her, and she melted with each and every touch. His lips were so giving, yet took as he pleased. She loved how he kissed her. His hands were soft as they cruised along sensitive skin, touching the bareness of her breasts.

She moaned when his mouth found her nipples and

teased them alive.

He gave her everything she could possibly ask for and more, and when he pressed himself inside of her, she exploded in a mind numbing orgasm.

And woke with tears in her eyes.

She cradled her body, still throbbing from her wet dream, and cried herself to sleep.

She did not dream of him again, but her sleep was not a restful one.

Chapter Thirteen

The place looked great. The walls were in a medium blue that shimmered when the night lights spun around from the dance floor. All the chairs were covered in red faux velvet and the tables had been replaced with dark oak that gleamed under the overhead lights. The dance floor was in black imitation marble that was as glossy as ice.

The bar had been refinished in a dark oak also, and all the stools were covered in red faux velvet. The pictures that hung on the walls were of famous baseball players, hockey players, and jerseys donated to him by famous teams. The glass behind the bar was smoked and lined with dark shelves filled with every type of alcohol available.

He was home.

Yet Justin felt a longing that hadn't been there before.

He missed his family, his friends, Beth.

Slipping behind the bar, Justin helped himself to a glass of scotch, then stood looking out over his bar.

His bar.

He'd run from his home, from his family, without a thought to what he would do on his own. He'd been eighteen, just out of high school, without any experience in the real world. If it hadn't been for his grandparents, he didn't know what he would have done.

Now, six years later, he owned his own bar, was in

the process of starting a restaurant for his mother, and earned enough money to live quite comfortably.

Yet he longed to be back home.

He downed the glass, then poured another. When the back entrance door clanked shut, Justin waited to see who had come in. Only his employees had the code, and when he saw Sara Edwards, the woman who managed his bar, stroll in, he downed his second glass.

"Oh, hey, you're back."

"So it seems. Place looks smokin'."

Setting her purse on the edge of the bar, Sara took a seat across the bar from where Justin stood and looked around the bar. "Doesn't it, though? They just finished two days ago. I was going to call and let you know today. But, well, here you are."

"Here I am." He poured another drink, only this time, let it sit on the bar.

"And from the tone in your voice and the bottle of scotch on the bar, I take it your trip home hadn't gone well."

"It went alright." Better than he'd thought.

"Then what's with the need to numb?" She tapped his glass with her long, red nails.

He'd known Sara for four years. When he'd first looked into opening a bar, he knew nothing about the business. So he'd hired a business consultant and Sara had been the girl. She'd run him through the process, helping him with everything, and when he'd finally had things in order, and realized he no longer needed her help, he'd taken her to his bed. They'd had a short but very hot relationship, and in the end, he offered her a job as his manager and she'd accepted. She still worked as a consultant, on the side, but for the most part, she worked in his bar. And he was glad to have her.

She was a petite brunette with a soft voice and a hard body. But despite her size, she knew how to handle herself, and she'd proven it several times when customers had gotten rowdy towards her.

"No real reason. I was thirsty. So, grand reopening

in two days. Are we ready?"

"You bet, and you're evading. What's up?"

He downed the glass of scotch before speaking. "Just a little homesick, I guess." Her burst of laughter startled him mainly because it had cackled out at a high pitch and echoed in the quietness of the room.

"You? homesick?" She continued to laugh, holding her ribcage.

His rolled his eyes and shook his head. "Yeah, too funny, and I'm the first to admit I never thought I would ever say those words, yet..." Here he was, feeling homesick.

"Well, isn't this interesting. Okay, tell me about your time in good old Passion?"

Walking around the bar, Justin pulled up a stool and sat beside her. "Condensed version. I was nearly arrested for refusal to pay a speeding ticket, by one of my old friends who is now a cop. I was released on a technicality, only to land back in jail that night with a black eye, cut lip, and a concussion thanks to another old friend."

"Some friend. I was going to ask about the bruised face."

"He blames me, apparently, because he went to jail for some crap after I left. So besides taking it out on me, he slashed my tires and spray painted some nasty shit on the hood of my car."

"Not the car," she gasped.

"It's been repaired and looks as good as new. I hung out with some old friends, spent time with my parents and sisters, and decided to start a restaurant for my mother in Passion."

Her brown eyes went wide and the corner of her mouth bowed in a grin. "Get out!"

"For real. And I think I might have some feelings for one of my old friends."

"Male or female?" When he glared at her, she chuckled and went on. "What's her name?"

"Beth Healy. We grew up together. She's over a

year older than me and in our youth, she and her brother Tyler and I were inseparable. As her younger brother grew up, he started hanging with us as well. But Beth and I, well, we were close."

"And now you have the hots for her. Did you sleep with her?"

"No," he sighed.

"Did you want to?"

"Yes." He stood up to pour himself another glass of scotch.

"And now I know the reason for the numb fest."

"I never got to say goodbye to her before I left."

"Ah."

"She's probably pissed at me for not saying goodbye."

"So call her."

Justin sighed, downed his glass of scotch. With the minimal amount of sleep he'd had and the lack of food in his belly, the alcohol was going straight to his head. "Yeah, I'll call her later. She's probably at work now." Setting the glass in the sink behind the bar, Justin walked to the stairs past the kitchen and headed up to his apartment.

He'd just catch some sleep before calling her.

~

"He called again."

Beth sat on the floor in her bedroom, packing up her belongings, pretending not to hear what her mother had just said.

"If you want to ignore Justin, that's fine, but I deserve more respect than that."

Feeling the guilt slap her as surely as if her mother's hand had, Beth apologized. "Sorry."

"Are you going to return any of the dozens of messages he's left since he headed out three weeks ago?"

"Nope." She stuffed the books from her nightstand into the box trying to fight off the sorrow she was feeling and had been feeling since Justin had left.

"I just don't understand why you're angry at him."

"Because he's a louse. I really don't want to talk about this anymore, Mom."

Her mother touched her arm and Beth nearly lost her control. "You're in love with him—"

"Mom, please." Biting her lip, Beth stood, hoisting the heavy box in her arms.

"Just talk to him. Call him back and talk to him."

"Why should I? Damn it, Mom, I didn't want to get into this." Her eyes burnt with tears she fought with. Setting the box on the bed, Beth collapsed beside it and wept. "He hurt me by leaving without saying goodbye."

"This time, or the last time?" her mother asked, sitting beside Beth, running a hand through her hair.

Beth sniffed. "This just reinforces the hurt from last time. He came to my room the night before he left and kissed me. He told me he wants me, then he leaves without a word. What am I supposed to feel about that?"

"Pissed." Her mother's voice echoed with anger.

"I was, at first, but now, now it just hurts. What was he hoping for, a quick roll with me before leaving, then go back to his pretty life and forget all about me? Damn him."

Her mother pulled out a tissue from the box on Beth's nightstand and wiped her tears. "I'm sorry sweetie."

"I knew he would do this, that's why I didn't give in to him. I knew he would leave me again and that would be it. God, Mom, I hate him so much, but I love him even more." She fell against her mother's shoulder, took comfort in the arms that came around her, sobbing with her pain.

~

The bar was jumping and packed to the gills with standing room only. It had been that way since he'd reopened the doors three weeks ago. Justin couldn't be happier, except…he wasn't. For three weeks he'd been calling Beth, and every time she was out. He'd left dozens of messages for her, none had been returned.

She was beginning to piss him off.

While in his office, Justin could hear the pumping music drum through the walls. It was a good beat, as was the norm in his establishment. Not like that drab country crap they'd played in Passions local bar.

Sitting at his desk, Justin took the yellow envelope before him, and tore it open. It was the paperwork and design plan for his mother's restaurant. Everything looked in order and would be set to break ground in a month. Perfect.

Picking up the phone on his desk, he called home to his parents. When Abby answered he blew out a breath of relief. "Hey sis, what's shaking?"

"Right now, the house. We're having a wicked early summer storm. Man, the lightning is lighting up the whole house."

His sister had never been a fan of storms. "You all alone?"

"Yeah. Mom and Dad are playing cards at the Healys'."

"Cool. So, is everything set?"

"Everything is ready to go."

"And she doesn't suspect a thing?"

"Nope." Abby giggled.

"What about Donna?"

"She'll be here."

"Good. Say, have you seen Beth lately?"

"Just today. Why?"

He tapped his finger on his desk while he spoke. "I've been trying to get a hold of her since I left. She's not returning my calls."

"Could be she's busy."

"Yeah, still... If you happen to see her...no, never mind. Catch you in a few, sis." He hung up the phone, then picked it right back up and dialed Beth's place one more time. When his Uncle Tom answered, Justin was a little disappointed. "Hey Uncle Tom, is Beth around?"

"No, she's not. Stop looking at my cards, Victor."

Justin bit his lip. His father was obviously trying to cheat, again. He missed being home even more now. "You know when she'll be home?"

"Can't say."

Justin huffed. "Well, when she does come, in can you tell her to return my calls already?"

"Will do."

Justin hung up, fuming.

Well, she wasn't going to be able to avoid him much longer.

~

"Justin?" Cassie asked when Thomas took his seat.

"Yep."

"He's going to keep calling until she talks to him."

"I know," Thomas agreed, lifting his cards.

"What did he do now?" Vic asked with a frown.

"Left without saying goodbye to Beth," Thomas added, throwing two cards on the discard pile.

"He intended to, but that means shit, doesn't it?" Vic let out a long breath. "When will he learn?"

"So she's just going to avoid him and not return his calls?" Julia wanted to know.

"Pretty much," Cassie shrugged.

Julia sighed. "Think we should let Justin know she's pissed at him?"

"I think that would be pretty obvious by her not returning his calls," Vic said, laying his hand over Julia's.

"Still, what if he doesn't know why she's mad?"

"Then it's up to her to tell him, or him to figure out. They're adults now; we can't keep stepping in when things get rough."

Julia gave Vic's a hand a squeeze. "You're right."

"She's in love with him," Cassie blurted out.

"What!" Vic and Julia said at once.

"You didn't know?" When they both shook their heads, she chuckled. "Guess blindness doesn't fall far from the tree. She has been for years, maybe always.

How could you two not see it?"

"Do you think maybe Beth didn't want anyone to know how she felt for Justin?" Thomas asked his wife, giving her a disapproving look.

Cassie just rolled her eyes. "It's not like Vic and Julia are going to go tell her they know."

"Damn." Vic rubbed a hand across his chin. "Now I get it."

"Bingo," Cassie replied with a snap.

"No wonder she's been so down at work lately."

"Love will do that to you," Cassie added.

"Especially when the other party doesn't reciprocate." Julia squeezed the bridge of her nose. "Our son is such a—"

"Dumbass?" Vic finished.

"I was going to say fool, but dumbass works just as well. So now what?"

"Now," Thomas dealt out the cards, "we finish our game."

Chapter Fourteen

Nothing much had changed in the month since he'd been gone. Other than the snow was completely gone now, and the trees were in full bloom, even the grass was starting to look lush. Spring had sprung into a glorious June.

Justin pulled into the parking lot of the local hotel, shutting off his car and engaging the alarm before heading to the front office. He'd phoned ahead to book his room and all he needed now was the key card. When he walked through the front doors, he cringed seeing Wes leaning on the desk. He could have just as easily done without seeing the likes of him any time soon.

He had a thought to turn around and come back later. Until the woman spoke up.

"Can I help you?"

So much for leaving. "I booked a room two day's ago. Justin Davis." When Wes turned around, the look in his eyes showed more than disdain.

"You're back."

"No, I'm a figment of your imagination. Ignore me." The guy was such a moron.

"Ah, here we go. Justin Davis, paid in full. You get room eight." She pulled a key card from the drawer and held it out to him.

"Thanks." He took the key and was more than eager to get the hell out of there.

"Room eight, huh? Maybe I'll pop by sometime

and have a chat."

"Save your breath for someone who cares," Justin spat while he exited the office. Was it too much to hope the guy had sprouted some decency and would actually leave Justin alone while he was in Passion?

Unlocking his room door, Justin entered to the fresh scent of cleaning liquid. It was so strong it burnt his nose. So he opened the window to let in some fresh air. Leaving the door open, Justin walked to his car to grab his luggage. When he entered his room, he found Wes sitting on his bed. He dropped his luggage, his face stern. "Get out."

"I just thought I would come by and say hi."

"Bullshit." The guy was full of it, and it showed not just in the sarcastic tone, but in the way he held himself. "Leave before I call the cops."

Wes stood, rotating his shoulders, then gave his coveralls a tug before sauntering to the door. "I wouldn't advise sticking around long."

"Is that a threat, Wes?"

He looked at Justin with those muddy brown eyes and smiled. "One you can take to the bank."

Justin slammed the door at his back and swore.

Welcome home.

~

First stop was his parent house to see his mother. Justin pulled up in the front and slid from his car. The sun was toasty warm today, and he felt it through the black short-sleeved button-down shirt he wore.

Walking up the path, he held his hand over his shoulder and engaged his car alarm. It beeped twice letting him know it was now locked. Stepping up to the door, he pressed the bell and waited. When the door opened to his mother on the other side, he felt the smile she sent back at him as if it had been placed on his heart.

"Surprise!"

"Oh, Justin!" She threw her arms around him and gave him a huge hug.

"Miss me?"

"And then some. What are you doing here? Not that I'm not glad."

He followed her into the living room and took a seat beside her on the sofa. "Like I said, surprise."

"That's it?"

"That's it." She just didn't know what the real surprise was yet.

"Well, I'm glad to see you." She leaned in and kissed his cheek. "Have you seen your father yet?"

"You're my first stop. I'll go see him in a bit. I would have liked to have been here for Mother's Day, but I just couldn't get away."

"I understand. I loved the flowers you sent me."

She'd always been a sucker for flowers of any kind. "Glad you liked them. I thought I could maybe take you and Dad out for dinner tomorrow. In the city."

"That's not necessary, but we would love to join you for dinner." She smiled slyly.

"Perfect. I'll book some place nice and let you know the time." He stood, taking her hands in his and drawing her to her feet. "It's really great to see you again."

"Miss me?" she teased.

"And then some."

~

Justin entered the police depot and felt a warmth in his gut at seeing Millie's familiar face sitting behind her desk. Her smile was infectious when she looked up at him, drawing out his own.

"Well, hello, handsome. Fancy seeing you again."

"I just couldn't stay away from you, Millie."

"I know it." She laughed. "So what brings you to town?"

"Like you don't know," He winked at her. "Is he in?"

"Just got back from a nasty car wreck. I was just about to bring him a cup of coffee, but since you're here, you can take it to him. Do you want one?" She stood and poured the cup.

"No thanks, Millie." Taking the cup she handed him to his father's office door, he knocked once before pushing the door open. He found his father leaning back in his seat, his hat off, a smoke dangling from one hand while the other one rubbed his eyes. He looked like he was completely worn out.

How many times had he seen that look on his father's face? Too many to count.

"Me thinks you're in need of this."

His father looked up, and the smile that filled his face warmed Justin's heart like nothing else had. "Justin. What are you doing here?"

"I was in the neighborhood and thought I'd drop in for coffee. You look beat."

"Rough car wreck. Thanks." He took the cup and instantly put it to his lips.

"Yeah, Millie was telling me. Any losses?"

"One, young boy. Seventeen. I'm sure his blood alcohol levels will be through the roof when the tox reports come back. He smelt like a brewery."

"What a shame."

"It never pays to drink and drive. Thank God he didn't take anyone with him. So, what's the real reason for your visit?" his father asked, tapping out his cigarette.

"I wasn't able to make it out for Mother's Day, so I thought I'd come out now and celebrate both Mother's Day and Father's Day, all in one."

His father nodded, swallowing his coffee. "That's nice."

"I want to take both you and Mom out for dinner tomorrow night. Some place in the city. You free?"

"I have tomorrow off, so yep, I'm free."

"Great. I told Mom I'd call and let her know what time." He stood and for the first time in…well, more years than he could remember, he felt satisfied with the visit with his father. There hadn't been the usual tension between them. "I'm staying at the hotel if you need to get a hold of me."

"Great."

Justin walked to the door, then paused. "Hey, is Beth working today?"

"No, she has today and tomorrow off."

"You know if she's at home?"

"Hers, probably."

Justin's head titled. "What do you mean by hers?"

"She bought a house a few weeks ago. She moved in yesterday."

He couldn't have been more shocked. "Really. Know the address?"

His father rattled off the address with a grin.

With the address in his head, Justin left his father's office and decided it was time he confronted Beth.

~

It was still sinking in. This was her house, her home. Hers. Beth stood in her sunken living room which had a direct view of the dining room and kitchen. She loved the open floor plan and the vaulted ceilings. It had been the open floor plan and the cedar that had drawn Beth in the most. That, and being at the top of the hill, looking down over the town. She would always be able to watch her town and protect it, even from her house.

Her ears picked up the sound of a vehicle on gravel, and when she walked to her front door, she saw a white Accord pulling into her driveway. Curious who it could be, Beth stepped out onto her veranda and waited for the person to exit the car.

When he did, her blood boiled and her heart ached.

"Look at you, living at the top of the hill like some high and mighty, looking down at the poor folk."

She slammed the door as she entered her house and threw the lock. He was not coming into her home.

"Come on, Beth, let me in."

"Go away, Justin." She jumped when he pounded his fists on the door.

"I'm not going away until we talk."

"I don't want to talk to you," she called out to him, her arms folded across her chest, her back straight in determination.

"So I gathered by all the unreturned phone calls. Either let me in or I'll break in."

"Then I'll have you arrested for breaking and entering." *See how you would like that.* When there was no reply, she walked to the door and peered out the peep hole. She frowned at not seeing him there, yet his car—or whosever car he was driving—was still in the driveway.

"Should have thought to lock the back door, too."

She jumped and let out a little screech as she spun to see Justin right behind her. The smile and laughter he spat out did not sit well with her. "Get out of my house."

"Not until we hash this out. Nice place, by the way. Love the vaulted ceilings."

"I'm glad my taste in homes is appealing to you." She crossed her arms over her chest again and glared at him. "Now get out."

"Why haven't you returned any of my calls?"

"Because I didn't want to talk to you."

"Well, duh, but why? You cut your hair."

She touched the ends that barely came to her chin. It had been a fleeting thought to chop all the locks off only because she kept remembering Justin's hands running though it. But now she regretted it.

"I like it better long."

So did she, but she wasn't about to tell him that. "Now that we've resolved the problem, you can leave."

"We haven't resolved anything. You still haven't told me why you're angry with me."

"Why do you think?" she spat at him, dropping her arms.

"If I knew that, I wouldn't have to ask," he said through gritted teeth.

"You leave town, twice, without telling me *or* saying goodbye. Excuse me if that pissed me off.

Happy? Now leave." She walked to the door only to have him grab her arm. Swiveling back towards him, she shot him a heated glare. "Remove it or lose it."

He dropped his hand but remained in his spot. "I tried, but you were out on patrol. What was I supposed to do, search for you?"

"You could have told me the night before that you were leaving. Or had you planned on taking me to bed, then running off with a satisfied grin on your face."

"What? Where the hell would you get that idea?"

"What else am I supposed to think?" Frustrated to hell, she walked off, needing to move before she exploded in rage.

"I don't know, maybe trust that I would never do that to you." She snorted. "What did that mean?"

"Just that." She grabbed a glass from the cupboard and stalked to the fridge for a drink of ice cold water. She needed something to cool her down.

"You honestly think I would do something like that to you?"

"In a heartbeat." When the silence filled the air, she looked over and saw him sitting at the table, looking down at his hands. Great, now he was sulking.

"You think that little of me?"

"You didn't give much reason to think otherwise." His head lifted and she continued. "You climb into the window in my bedroom, grab me and kiss me and act like you're going to take me right there, no questions asked. You had arrogant ass written all over you."

He looked down at his hands again.

Feeling like crap now, buddy? Good. She stood in her kitchen, leaning against the counter, sipping her water while Justin sat in the chair, not saying a word. Several minutes passed before he finally spoke up.

"I guess I did give off that sort of vibe." She snorted again and had his brow raising. "Okay, I was an arrogant ass. But I meant what I said before I left. We're not finished."

"Oh, yes we are." She set her glass in the sink then

walked to the front door. Pulling it open, she waited.

He stood, walking slowly, casually, towards her. When he stopped directly in front of her, she sucked in a breath. "I know what I felt when I kissed you, Beth. It was reciprocal."

"Don't start this again." When he lifted his hand and his fingers grazed her cheek, she was defenseless. Her eyes closed and she sighed.

"See."

She felt him lean in towards her and the instant his lips touched hers, she wanted to throw it all away and give in. But this was Justin, and he was bound to keep hurting her.

"Kiss me back, Beth," he whispered against her mouth.

"No." God, how she wanted to.

"You want to and we both know it."

He was nibbling on her lips, making them tingle, making her whole body tingle. She opened her eyes and that had been a major mistake. His eyes were so blue, so sincere that she felt herself drowning in them. And when his tongue skimmed over her bottom lip, she dove.

His fingers threaded through her hair as he drew her closer. His mouth took hers in such a sweet kiss she thought she might cry. There was gentleness yet a needy desire in this kiss, and when she felt herself drowning, she was reminded of the man she was going down with.

She pushed him away, grabbed his arm and shoved him through the door. She locked the door even before he had a chance to speak.

"What the hell, Beth!"

"It's wrong; we're wrong. This can't happen." The tears flowed down her cheeks.

"Why the hell not?"

"Because," she spat out, then whispered the rest, "you'll only leave me in pain."

~

Justin stood by the door, the sound of her tearful confession ripping a hole in his heart. He left the door to walk down the steps to his car. He felt sore inside, like someone had punched a hole through his chest. Climbing into his rental car, Justin looked up to see Beth standing by the living room window. Her hand came up and he thought for a moment she would wave goodbye. Then she swiped her fingers across her cheek and he knew she'd just brushed her tears aside.

Damn it. She was crying over him.

Chapter Fifteen

Justin pulled up to his parents' house at just past six. Dressed in a tailored black suit and navy blue tie, Justin climbed from his car to walk to the front door. He didn't wear a suit often, and the last time he had, had been at his grandfather's funeral. This time, however, was a joyous occasion. At least he hoped it would be.

With a quick tap of his knuckles on the front door, Justin stepped inside the house. There was the ever present scent of food in the house that he equated with is mother that brought a smile to his lips. Apparently, she'd done some baking today.

"I hope you're ready to go, because I'm famished," Justin called out, wondering where they could possibly be.

"We'll be down shortly."

"Well, hustle your butts," Justin shouted up to his father, huffing at their lateness. His hands in his suit jacket pockets, Justin wandered the tiny house he'd once called home. The pictures of the family were still on the fireplace mantel, and Justin frowned at his last school picture. Man, what had he been thinking with the hair. His blond hair had been shaved around the base and longer on top, spiked at least two inches high. And tipped in green. Lord, those had been bad hair days. He rather preferred his cut the way it was now. Short all around and just a bit longer on top, swept to the side. No green.

The clock over the mantel showed ten after six now. If his parents didn't hurry, they were going to be more than a little fashionably late. When he heard the first sound of footsteps on the stairs, he saw his father, dressed in a deep brown suit and red tie—of which he was still fastening around his neck—hurry down the steps.

"You have a situation at work that kept you late?"

"Nope," His replied, adjusting his collar.

Justin frowned, then glanced back at the stairs to see his mother hurrying down, smoothing out her skirt. "What the—oh, Lord. You guys were—"

"You want me to drive?" his father inquired, obviously trying to change the subject.

"I can't believe the two of you. I told you I would be here at six, sharp, and you're up there doing...God!" He shuddered. The idea that he might have walked in on them having sex sent shivers down his spine. Sure, he knew his parents had a sex life, and a healthy one from what he remembered—and that brought on a whole pile of horrible memories in itself—but still, at their age, enough was enough.

"Abby was gone, and we had the house to ourselves—which is a rarity—and your father always looks so good in a suit—"

"Stop, please, my ears." He clasped his hands over his ears, shaking his head. He so didn't want to hear the details or the whys. "I'll drive." Letting out a long breath, Justin walked to the door.

"Is this a new car?" his mother asked, climbing into the passenger side, on the insistence of her husband.

"It's a rental. I flew in this time." Justin explained, starting the engine and sending them rolling. So they'd be a little late. No problem. "I didn't have as much time to drive out this time."

"Oh, I see. Who is looking after the bar while you're gone?"

"My manager, Sara. She's great, a gem really. Don't know what I would do without her."

"That's great, that you have someone you can rely on. So how long will you be staying?"

"A week." He signaled and headed out onto the highway. Soon, very soon his mother would have her gift. He couldn't wait to see her reaction.

"And you're staying at the hotel again?"

"Yep. Room eight."

"Well, it certainly is nice to have you home again," his mother expressed, and laid her hand on Justin's as it rested on the stick shift.

Wasn't it odd that he would feel the same? It was nice to be home.

~

He'd reserved one of the banquet areas, and he'd been told it was at the back of the restaurant. When they entered the elegant restaurant, Justin gave his name and was instantly lead through the busy crowd of diners. He could only imagine his parents' thoughts when they kept going further back.

"Here we are," the petite waitress spoke, standing beside the double doors.

"Thank you." Justin gave her a fresh smile. Then took hold of the door's brass handles and pulled them open.

"Surprise!" The crowd cheered, startling both his parents.

"What on earth?" his mother gasped.

"Belated Happy Mother's Day and early Happy Father's Day." The look on his parents' faces was of utter shock.

"Well, hell," his father exclaimed, rubbing a hand across his chin.

Not only were both his sisters there, but everyone of the Healy's had shown up. The youngest, Tommy Healy, making enough noise for all of them. Millie was there because she'd always been a part of their family.

"He's hungry," Lissy explained while she cradled her son to her breast.

"He isn't the only one. You guys are late," Donna

stated, giving Justin an evil look.

"Don't blame me. They had to have a quickie before I showed up."

"God, you guys." Rolling her eyes, Donna grabbed hold of her father's arm and led him to the table, while Justin took his mother's.

"You are a sneaky bunch." His mother wagged her finger at her children and her friends. "No one said a word."

"Hence the surprise. It's not over yet, though," Justin added, holding the chair for his mother. "Open the envelope." He pointed to the yellow envelope on the table before her, his excitement rising.

His mother looked over at her husband, who only shook his head. She took the envelope and tore it open. As she pulled the blueprints out, her brow curled in confusion. "I'm not sure I understand."

"That," Justin started, taking a seat beside her. "Is the blueprints for your new restaurant. Julia's." He pointed to a section on the blueprint. "And that is Vic's Lounge."

The silence from both his parents was not what he expected. But then he supposed they needed time to look it over and to let it all sink in.

"Well, what do you think?"

"You're building a restaurant and lounge?" Julia finally asked.

"Yep, for you, right in Passion."

"I don't understand."

He touched her cheek with his fingertips and smiled. "You are the greatest cook I have ever known. You deserve your own place where people can come in and sample your finest cuisine. And I know how much you love cooking and baking. Now you can do it all the time, for everyone."

"Holy hell, Julia!" Cassie exclaimed from across the table.

"I don't know the first thing about running a restaurant, Justin."

"You won't be running it alone. I plan on hiring a manager to help you get started. Besides, you'll be too busy cooking."

"Am I supposed to be working in the bar?" his father asked in a sober voice.

"No, well, not unless you want to. It's your call." Why did they not seem more excited about this? "I just wanted to give you both a place of your own."

"Isn't that exciting, Mom and Dad?" Abby asked, her face aglow.

"It is definitely something." His father laid the blueprints down then leaned back in his seat, his eyes glossy.

Justin was disappointed and he was sure it showed on is face. But hell, he'd expected a little more happiness from his parents. "Anyone want some champagne?" Reaching for the bottle, Justin popped he cork, desperately needing a drink. He poured everyone a glass then held his up for a toast. "To my parents." He just didn't have anything else to say. Damn it, he was upset.

As glasses clinked, he sat down and wished desperately for the evening to be over.

~

Heading back to Passion, Justin was glad Abby and Donna were driving his parents back home. He didn't think he could handle being in the car with them after getting such a disappointing response. The meal had trudged on endlessly and Justin conversed with everyone, but he was sure they all saw that his feelings had been hurt.

It was just before midnight when he pulled onto the road leading into Passion. He wasn't in the mood to go back to the hotel, so he kept driving and found himself pulling up the hill to Beth's house.

She hadn't said much to him all evening, and each time he'd looked at her, she'd looked away. He hated that there was a wedge between them and was determined to fix it. He just wasn't sure how.

Coming to a stop in her driveway, he climbed from his car and headed up the steps to her front door. It really was a nice place, rustic with a pinch of modernization. The veranda covered the entire front part of the house, and he could easily imagine a white wooden table and chairs near the east side of the house, with baskets of flowers hanging from the rail that lined the deck.

And wasn't it odd that he could imagine himself sitting at that table, drinking his first morning coffee with Beth beside him.

Turning back to the door, he pressed the bell and waited. When the door finally opened and he saw Beth standing before him in a pair of gray sweats and white t-shirt, he had the strongest urge to sweep her into his arms and carry her to bed.

He was pretty damn sure she wouldn't be impressed by that.

"Hey."

"Hey," she replied.

"I wasn't in the mood to go back to my hotel room alone. Can I come in?" She seemed to hesitate before stepping aside. "Thanks. You changed?" She'd worn a neat black skirt and white shirt with lace along the front. She'd looked so pretty, and he didn't mind admitting that he'd admired her long, shapely legs when she'd stood from her seat. She really had matured into a beautiful woman.

"No point keeping the outfit on at home. I was going to head to bed soon."

"Oh. Do you work early tomorrow?" He really didn't want to leave yet.

"Not until noon."

"And you're going to bed already?" He took a seat on the leather sofa and admired her taste. Every piece of furniture in the room was in black leather. She had throw cushions of bright red on the couch and a red faux fur rug on the hardwood floor. It really was a nice set up, very close to his own living room back home.

"I usually try to keep a regular schedule, but since I had coffee so late, I'm a little wired still. I thought you'd be spending time with your family."

She took a seat in the chair across from him, curling her legs beside her and he noticed her feet were bare. She had cute feet, and the nails were painted a blood red. Come to think of it, red was her favorite color. "They were wiped. I'm used to late nights. I usually go to bed at about five in the morning and sleep until noon or two."

"I hate when I work the night shifts. I just can't get to sleep in the morning."

"I suppose it would be harder to get used to if you had swing shifts. My shifts are always the same."

"Do you run the bar?"

He shrugged out of his suit jacket and loosened his tie. The damn thing was strangling him. "I'm always present in the bar, but Sara runs it for the most part."

"Sara?"

"My manager."

"Oh." She fiddled with her toes.

"I'm usually in the bar every night, but some nights I just check out the late night crowd then go to my office and do paperwork. My staff is pretty capable and usually run the place just fine without me."

"I have to admit, I never would have pictured you as a bar owner. An owner of any business, really. You hated math."

"Still do, that's what accountants are for," he laughed, sliding down in his seat, getting comfortable.

"And now you're starting this restaurant for your parents. Quite something."

"I thought so. Though, I don't know that my parents are as happy about it."

"Of course they are. And why wouldn't they be? You'll be around more often now."

He would be, for a while at least, until the place got its footing. "They just didn't seem that…enthused about it."

She uncurled her legs only to curl them to the other side. "It was a huge shock. They just need time to get used to the idea."

"I suppose so." He hadn't really thought of it that way. "Will you be?"

She tilted her head to the side. "Will I be what?"

"Happy to have me around more often?" The pause was enough to make him worry.

"It'll be nice to see more of you, sure."

"I sense hesitation there."

She shrugged, played with her toes again.

"What is it? Just say it."

"I don't want you thinking there's a chance for us."

He tilted his head back in surprise. "Why not?"

"I'm not going to be your fling while you're here, Justin."

"Did I say you would be?"

"What else would I be?"

He didn't like the way she was thinking. "My friend."

"If that's all you want, then fine."

"It's not all I want, Beth, and you know it."

"And that's why I'm telling you now that that's all I'll be. If you want a quick lay while you're in town, I'm sure someone will be able to accommodate you."

"Jesus, Beth. What do you think I am?" He stood now, moving towards her. "I don't want anyone else. Why can't we see where we could go if we got together?"

"Because long distance relationships never work out."

"I'll be here often enough for the first while, enough to spend some serious time with you."

"Oh, why, thank you. How nice of you to allow me some serious time."

His brow curled in his frustration. "That wasn't what I meant. I simply meant that—"

"It doesn't matter. I'm not interested. I think it's

time you left." She stood and, skirting around him, walked to the front door.

"You know, just once I would like to finish our conversations before you kick me out."

"This conversation is finished." She opened the door, held it.

"Not by a long shot, sweetheart." And to prove to her he was anything but through with her, he yanked her towards him in one quick move that left her stunned, then plastered his mouth to hers. It might have been a quick kiss, but it was no less potent. He wanted to leave a point.

Walking to his car, his hand jingling the keys in his pocket, Justin was determined to change her mind.

They could work out just fine.

Chapter Sixteen

There was a floral shop in Passion. There had never been one before. And on top of it being a floral shop, it was also a greenhouse. Well, hell, Passion had progressed. Would wonders never cease?

It was perfect; at least he didn't have to drive into the city for what he wanted. And hopefully the shop would have everything he needed. Entering the shop, a faint chime from an electronic alarm system announced his arrival. The door had barely closed when a tall brunette strode up to him with a bright red smile. She looked to be about forty, and with all that dark make-up caked on, his guess was she was in denial about her true age. Make-up didn't make a person look young; well that was his thoughts in it in any case. The sale lady obviously didn't hold his belief.

"Good afternoon, how may I help you today?"

Oh lord, she even had one of those squeaky annoying voices. "I'm looking to purchase some flowers. Indoor and outdoor."

"And what a perfect time to plant. Was there anything in particular you were looking for?"

"Not really. I'm kinda clueless in the flower department. I know she likes red, though, so anything red would be great."

"Ah, for a lady. Okay, what sort of flower does she prefer?"

Justin shrugged. "Beats me." Even racking his brain,

thinking back to their past, Justin couldn't remember Beth ever mentioning a favorite flower. Did she even like flowers? Right. What woman didn't like flowers?

"Okay. Annuals or perennials?"

"Huh?"

She laughed, and though he hadn't thought it possible, her voice went even higher. "Annuals are seasonal. They stick around only while the season lasts, then die off. Perennials come back every year, so it saves having to replant every spring."

"Can you have these perennials in pots?"

"Usually, no. They thrive better in the ground. Are you looking for potted plants?"

"Yeah. I was thinking of something that could hang off a balcony."

"Alright, why don't we go to the garden area and see what we can find."

An hour later he'd picked out enough flowers to line the entire veranda and then some. Plus, he'd purchased a bouquet of an assortment of flowers in a huge vase. He hoped Beth liked them. He'd scheduled the outdoor plants for delivery later today. He couldn't wait to see her face when she came home to fresh flowers lining her property entrance. The bouquet would be delivered to her at work.

He was going to convince her they could work, even if it meant buying out the damn floral shop to do it.

~

They'd been called to a domestic dispute on an acreage that had turned ugly in the blink of an eye. A child, Barry Grant, had called, crying and pleading for help and through his sobs; he told the dispatcher that he was scared his daddy was going to kill his mommy.

When Beth and three of her fellow officers arrived on the scene, they'd seen just how bad the situation was. The wife's face was a mess of blood and bruises, the front of her shirt coated in blood. The husband had been reluctant to let them in, when he'd come to the door. But when his ten year old son, Barry, had rushed out from behind him asking for help, they'd insisted on entering. That's when they'd seen the wife. She could barely stand, and the bastard husband was insisting she'd fallen down the stairs.

When they'd pressed her on it, she had only whimpered and nodded her head in agreement with her husband.

That's when it had all gone out of control.

The boy had started screaming, "Liar, liar," at his father. And when she and her fellow officers looked back at the frantic boy, they saw the rifle in his arms. It looked so huge against his tiny body, but he seemed to know how to handle it. And before any of them could speak a word to get him to set it down, he fired.

The shot hit his father in the gut, taking him down fast.

Constables Grady and O'Malley had jumped on the boy, removing the weapon from his hands. He had kicked and he'd screamed and he'd demanded to know if his father was dead. Then he'd collapsed and the tears had flowed.

"I had to do it. He would have killed my mom if I didn't," he'd sobbed and had shown his true age then.

Beth had held him while her partners tended to the victims, and when O'Malley shook his head at her, indicating the father hadn't made it, she cradled Barry a little tighter.

This was not something a child of his age should ever have to deal with.

She'd stayed with Barry until child services had arrived. At his insistence, she sat with him while the woman, Mary Bells, told him where he would be staying for the night. He hadn't liked the idea of being apart from his mother, but understood that she needed to be cared for in the hospital.

When Beth had helped him into Mary's car, he had asked then, if his father was alive. When Beth had told him no, he nodded his head and said simply, "Now we're safe."

God, what kind of world did they live in that a ten year old had to grow up in such a destructive home and felt the only way out of it was to kill his father. It sickened her.

Thank God it had been near the end of her shift. If she'd had to work an entire shift, even half a shift, following that incident, she just might not have made it. When she entered the depot, Beth was surprised by the bouquet of flowers that had been delivered for her. And when she'd seen who they'd been from, it both brightened her mood and saddened it all the same.

Beth knew why he'd sent them, and it hurt to know she had to let him down.

She simply didn't want her heart broken by him.

At just past one, she pulled up her driveway and let out a long suffering sigh. Justin's car was parked in her driveway. She really didn't want to see him right now. Grabbing her hat, Beth slid from her car and began walking towards her house. The scent caught her first, then she saw the flowers. Or rather, the garden of flowers taking up residence along her walkway and on her veranda. As she stepped up the deck, she was in awe of the plethora of posies that hung from the wooden deck along the front of the veranda. Red and white petunias and red carnations. It was breathtakingly beautiful.

Then she saw Justin sitting at a white table near the east side of the veranda and she crumbled.

"Do you like them?"

She sobbed like a baby, falling to her knees on the wooden floor, cradling her belly as it ached from the destruction she'd been witness to the past three hours.

"What the hell?" He ran to her, falling at her side, touching a hand to her face. "Beth, what's wrong? Are you sick?"

She only shook her head and fell into his arms. She didn't know how long she cried but she felt drained when she was finally finished. If there was an ounce of fluid left in her body after her crying jag, she would be surprised.

He wiped her damp face with his hand and her heart gave.

"What's the matter? Talk to me."

Being in his arms felt good, so right, she wished she could stay there forever. She knew that was impossible, but for one night at least, maybe she could have him. She needed desperately to feel something other than this horrid despair. "Take me to bed, Justin. Make love to me."

"Beth—"

"Please," Beth pleaded and she knew how desperate she sounded. She didn't care. Right now, she felt utterly desperate. And to show him she meant what she asked for, she took his face in her hands and kissed him with a greedy need that shocked even her.

He scooped her into his arms and carried her into her house. When he set her down in her bedroom, she wasted no time on formalities and began disrobing him.

"Slow down," he panted.

"Faster." She needed to feel, now. Yanking his shirt open, she ran her short nails along his bare chest while her mouth devoured the soft meaty flesh of his earlobe. God, he smelt good. Spicy, yet floral.

More, she wanted more. Yanking at the belt around his waist, she couldn't wait to feel him in her hands. When he finally managed to get her uniform shirt unbuttoned, he paused and she realized she still wore her vest.

"You wear this all the time?"

"When I'm called to a domestic dispute." She yanked her shirt off then pulled the Velcro tabs to release the bullet-proof vest. It was meant to protect her, but right now it was hampering her. When she finally pulled it free, she breathed in a huge breath.

Tossing it aside, she made busy work removing her belt which held her gun, baton, and handcuffs. When she was finally free of that, she went back to working on Justin.

"What the hell has gotten into you?"

"You want me to stop?" She wouldn't even if he said yes.

"Hell, no!" He laughed, tugging at his zipper.

"Then shut up." Shoving her hands into his pants, she was surprised that he wore nothing beneath his trousers. Damn, that was hot.

"Oh, Jesus," he gasped when she grabbed hold of him.

"Touch me!" Beth demanded, then nibbled on his earlobe. He didn't waste any time unclasping her bra. His hands cupped her breasts, squeezing, teasing, tormenting. The fire erupted inside of her, demanding to be sated. God, she wanted his hands all over her body and when one hand slipped from her breast to her waist, she held her breath. As he slid her pants down, she gripped him even harder.

"Jesus, Beth, you're going to make me come."

"That would be the goal." But she lost her grip on his shaft when his hand dove beneath her underwear and touched her heat. The fire that had been burning inside of her spread, and when he speared her with his fingers, the heat exploded in an inferno.

"Oh, God, yes," she cried out, her head falling back while he worked his fingers inside of her with piston action.

"I have to have you, now," he demanded, pulling his fingers free. Kicking out of his pants, he hoisted her up and set her on the bed, then shoved her down.

She felt him move by the bed and when she looked down she saw him slip a condom on. It was the most erotic thing she had seen in a long time. She realized when she bent her legs at the knees that she still wore her boots. She began kicking them off and was grateful when Justin unlaced them for her.

"Take me. Now!" He spread her legs apart, then plunged. She let out a cry, her body catapulted into an earth shaking orgasm that seemed to last forever. He pumped into her with hard thrusts making the bed shake. She wanted more. "Harder."

"You want it harder?"

"Yes," she panted, her back arched, her body aching with a need she couldn't understand. "Now." He pulled free, flipped her onto her belly then lifted her hips. She braced herself on her elbows and when he penetrated her, her eyes nearly crossed. It was a shock to her system, but a pleasant one. She gripped the bedding and rode the torturous pounding he was giving her.

When his hand came around her and began playing with her nub, her body reacted in the appropriate manner. Beth began to move with the rhythm of his fingers, of his hips. She hadn't thought she had anything left in her to give and was surprised by how wrong she was. The orgasm that hit her came on sharp and ricocheted throughout her body. He twitched inside of her while he came with his release.

Exhausted, she collapsed on the bed, Justin falling on top of her.

"Holy fuck."

She couldn't agree more, but she was too damn tired to express it. As her eyelids drooped and her body throbbed, she drifted off to sleep while Justin rested inside of her.

~

Justin slipped himself out of Beth and pulled off the condom. Since the room was pitch black and he couldn't see worth a damn, he slid from the bed and made his way to the door. He stubbed his toe on something hard that felt like wood. Probably her dresser. Hissing quietly, so not to wake Beth, he hobbled from the room. Spotting the washroom to his left, he entered the room and tossed the condom in the trash can.

He emptied his bladder, then washed his face and hands before slipping back into Beth's bed. She was still in the exact position he'd left her in. Face down, legs spread, arms splayed out across the bed, head to the side. He'd left the bathroom light on, and with the light illuminating the room, he stood and admired the beauty before him.

She certainly had a body, and she knew how to use it. Damn, she had practically worn him out.

What had come over her? If he had known buying her flowers would result in her fucking him to near death, he would have done it long ago.

"Come on sleeping beauty." Carefully sliding his hand beneath her head and shoulders, he shifted her, swinging her so she was in the right position on the bed. She moaned, crawled to her side of the bed, which also happened to be his side of preference and stayed fast asleep. She slept like the dead.

Shifting her, he pulled the blanket out from under her, then covered her up, but not before admiring the length of her and the soft golden fur at the top of the V between her legs. It was the only hair present; she was as smooth as a baby everywhere else. And as he looked down at her, he could see the moisture glistening the soft supple skin between her legs.

Shaking his head, he tore his eyes free and pulled the blanket over her. If he'd have kept looking any longer, he would have been tempted to spread her wide and drive himself into all that dampness.

Instead, he slid between the sheets and curled in beside her. As she slept soundly beside him, he played with her golden hair.

He really wished she hadn't cut it.

Chapter Seventeen

Oh, lord, her body ached. When Beth awoke, every inner muscle throbbed. She felt used, abused, and utterly satisfied.

Rolling over, she saw Justin sound asleep beside her. She closed her eyes and regretted her actions.

What had she done?

What hadn't she done? She'd thrown herself at him, demanding to be taken, and taken she had been. She'd never had sex that roughly before. It was so unlike her; she didn't understand what she had been thinking.

She hadn't been. All Beth had wanted was to feel something other that hopeless despair. Well, she'd accomplished that, hadn't she? The orgasms she'd experience with Justin had been mind numbing. Nothing like she'd ever felt before. And where had the need to be pounded so hard come from? Normally she liked it soft, gentle. She liked to make love, not fuck.

As he rolled onto his side, facing away from her, she noticed the tattoo on his left shoulder blade. It was a skull spitting flames. Odd, she thought, then she saw the one on his arm. She sat up, looking a little closer at the Grim Reaper tattoo on his upper bicep.

The Justin she remembered never would have gotten a tattoo. He hated needles and despised pain. Yet here he was, sporting two rather large-sized tattoos. She wondered if he'd been sedated while the ink had been spread beneath his skin.

"The skull was a dare. Once I had that one done, I had to get the reaper," he said, rolling onto his back. "Good morning, beautiful."

She pulled away, regret weighing heavily on her shoulders. "I thought you hated needles." He'd gone all white in the face when the doc had mentioned stitching his lip.

"I do, but this is different. It's for a purpose. You have mascara under your eyes." He reached out to wipe the smudges, but she pulled away before he could touch her.

She didn't want him touching her. Grabbing her uniform shirt, she slipped it on, then rose from the bed to hurry to the washroom. God, she looked horrid. The mascara was more than smudged; it was running down her cheeks, probably from her crying jag. Had he been teasing her about being beautiful? More than likely.

She scrubbed her face clean, then sat down on the floor and took a deep breath.

Now what was she supposed to do?

"Beth?"

She jumped and was damn glad he hadn't seen it. "What?"

"Are you okay?"

"Just dandy."

"You don't sound dandy. Talk to me."

"I need to shower and get ready for work. Help yourself to…whatever in the kitchen before you leave." She hoped he would be gone by the time she was done in the shower.

When the door opened, she cursed herself for not locking it. She jumped into the shower, pulling the curtain closed and had just started up the water by the time he entered the room.

"You were pretty shaken up last night. Wanna tell me about it?"

"No." She just wanted him to leave so she could wallow in her misery. When he pulled the shower curtain aside, she actually yelped. "What the hell are you doing?"

"Looking you in the face while you lie to me. Why won't you tell me what's wrong?"

"Look, I had a rough night. No biggie."

His eyebrows arched. "Oh, sweetheart, it was most definitely something. You were a mess last night. Was it seeing all the flowers? Don't like them? Because if you don't, I can take them back?"

She yanked the curtain closed, wanting an ounce of dignity. "It wasn't the flowers." She vaguely remembered what they looked like.

He thrust the curtain back and she growled at him. "Then what was it?"

"I said I don't want to talk about it, okay. Now if you don't mind, I would like to continue my shower and get ready for work before I'm late." She closed the curtain, keeping her fingers crossed that he gave up and left. When he did, she blew out a long breath then stepped under the spray.

How the hell was she supposed to look at him after the way she had behaved the night before? She was embarrassed by her behavior. Embarrassed with the fact that she had used him to ease the pain in her heart she'd been feeling for the family that she'd seen crumble before her.

When she heard her front door slam shut, she was both grateful and saddened by his leaving.

She stood beneath the streaming hot water and let her tears fall.

~

Justin had gone back to his hotel room to shower and change before heading to his father's office. He had to know what had happened with Beth the night before, and since she'd been working, he figured his father would know if anything had happened with her.

"Good morning, Justin."

He tipped his head to Millie, glancing over at his father's door. "Hey, is my dad in?"

"Sure. Go on in. He's going over last night's reports."

"Thanks." He knocked once on the door before stepping in. "Got a minute?"

"Sure." His father waved Justin in, then focused on the folders on his desk. "Rough one last night." He taped the file.

"That's why I'm here. Did something happen to Beth last night?"

His father leaned back and lit a cigarette. "Why do you ask?"

Justin took the chair and sitting down, rested his ankle on his knee. "She came home last night and burst into tears. She was barely consolable."

"You were with her last night?"

"Yes, and before you ask, yes, all night. Something happened to her and I want to know what it was."

His father drew heavily on his cigarette before replying. "She responded to a domestic dispute."

"And…"

"And it was a rough one."

"You have to give me more than that."

"No, actually, I can't."

"Come on, Dad, cut the bureaucracy crap and just give it to me straight. Was she hurt?"

"Not in the physical from. What did she say to you?"

"Nothing, that's why I'm here."

"You said she was inconsolable. How bad was she?"

"She crumbled. This morning when I tried to get her to talk to me, she shut me down. Now tell me what went down."

His father tapped out his cigarette before responding. "She, along with three of my other officers, responded to a domestic dispute last night. Long story short, the ten year old son picked up his fathers rifle and blew a hole in his old man's gut. Right in front of Beth."

"Jesus."

"It was her first death."

"Christ. No wonder she fell apart." Justin rubbed a hand across his face.

"I'll get her to see the counselor when she comes in. If it affected her that deeply, she needs to work it out before I can send her back out in the field."

"Good." Justin stood, feeling better now that he knew why Beth had been so upset.

"Can I ask you a question?"

"Sure." Justin slid his hands in his jeans pockets.

He fidgeted in his seat, cleared his throat then spoke. "What is the real reason behind building this restaurant for your mother?"

"Exactly what I said the other night. She deserves it. She's a phenomenal cook, and I think it's about time she shared it with everyone."

Vic nodded but he didn't seem satisfied by Justin's response.

"What?"

"Well, it's just... If you did it out of guilt—"

"Guilt? What the hell do you mean by that?" Justin barked.

"Never mind." His father waved him off.

"No, say it. You've gone this far, just spit it out."

"Okay, fine." He stood now so he was eye-level with Justin. "Your mother and I feel like it's a conciliatory gift."

"You think I'm trying to buy my forgiveness?" He was appalled.

"Well...I shouldn't have said anything."

"Fuck that!"

"Justin!"

"Christ. I try to do something nice and this is the thanks I get. I decided on doing this the day before I left last time I was here. Mom was busy making food for some anniversary she was catering and it just clicked. She loves cooking, so I thought the perfect thing would be if she had a place of her own to do it in. A place where others could come and enjoy what she created. No, it wasn't a fucking guilt buy. She deserves to have her own fucking place. I'm out of here."

"Well, what the hell are we supposed to think, Justin?" he responded, stopping Justin as he walked to the door.

"You're supposed to think your son was doing something kind and nothing more. But why should I expect you would think I had no ulterior motive. You never fucking trusted me, why start now."

"You're right, I never did trust you, and you gave me plenty of reason not to trust you."

"Screw this. I don't need to stand here and be persecuted. Again."

"That's right, run away. It's what you do best. You're a man now, Justin, time to start acting like one."

Justin spun around, fury lacing his words. "That's right, Dad, I am a man now. But you can't see that, can you? All you see when you look at me is disappointment *My son failed me*. That's what you think when you look at me. Well, here's news, *Dad*, did you ever think the reason why I rebelled was because I could never match the expectations you set for me."

"What expectations? To be a decent human being?" his father spat back.

"I was a boy, you wanted a man, and now that I am a man, you still aren't satisfied."

"I never wanted you to be a man."

Justin snorted in disgust. "The hell you didn't. You kept pushing your profession at me, trying to groom me for a life as a cop when you knew damn well I resented you being a cop."

He stepped back as if Justin had ploughed his fist in his gut. "I…you resented my profession?"

"Don't act so surprised."

"I am surprised. Why?"

Justin blew out a breath, scratched his head in frustration. "You were rarely around when I needed you. Mom was the one who attended class meetings, soccer games, baseball tournaments. I would hear you come home from a rough night and talk to Mom about it. I heard all the horror you endured, all the crap people tried to pull, and I hated that you continued to walk out the door and protect people you didn't even know. I always feared you would never come home again."

"I had no idea."

"No, because you never bothered to really look at me. I don't want to do this now." Spinning on his heels, Justin left his father's office and nearly plowed into Beth. He didn't say a word because he was too furious. Instead he just kept going.

~

Utterly confused, Beth walked to Vic's door and knocked.

"Enter." He called out and the tone in his voice implied his meeting with Justin had not gone well. She entered the office to find him standing by his window, a hand in his hair. That was always a sure sign of stress in Vic. "You okay?"

He nodded. "I'm glad you stopped in before heading out on patrol. We need to talk about last night."

She really didn't want to get into it again. "Okay."

"Have a seat." He held his hand out to the chair, which wasn't a good sign.

Beth took the seat, her body tense.

"I read over the report from last night. How are you dealing with it?"

She shrugged, removed her hat and rested it on her knee. "Alright," she lied.

Vic laced his fingers and rested them on his desk. "That's not what Justin says."

She narrowed her eyes. "What did he tell you?" God help him if he'd told Vic they'd spent the night together.

"That you broke down last night after coming home. It's okay, Beth. It's a natural response, given the circumstances."

"I'm fine," she emphasized and in her mind pictured wrapping her hands around Justin's neck and squeezing the life out of him.

"I'd like you to see the counselor just to be sure."

"What?" She stood up abruptly, her hat falling to the floor. She bent to pick it up, still furious. "I don't need to see the shrink."

"It isn't a request, Beth. You know the rules when it comes to firing a weapon—"

"I didn't fire my weapon," she stated vehemently.

"No, but a weapon was discharged in your presence. You witnessed a little boy kill his father, Beth. You don't walk away from that untouched."

"I wasn't untouched, but I dealt with it."

Vic remained in his seat but told her not just with his words, but with his tone and his eyes also. He wasn't backing down. "Until you see the counselor, I don't want you on active duty."

"That's just bullshit—" She clamped her mouth shut, realizing who she was talking to. Sure, he was her uncle, but on the job, he was her superior. She needed to respect that. "Beg pardon, sir. But—"

"No buts, Constable Healy. Report to Millie and have her set up an appointment."

"Yes, sir." She saluted him, then stiffly spun around and marched from the room. It was crap; she was more than capable of being back on duty. She was going to kill Justin for mentioning her momentary lapse the night before.

She reported to Millie who called the official counselor, and by the time Beth left the office with her appointment booked, she was steaming mad.

~

Justin had taken time to cool his head after leaving his father's office, but not so much that he wasn't still somewhat pissed off. Okay, mostly hurt. And who wouldn't be? The things his father had implied stung, not because they were the truth, which they weren't, but because he'd only wanted to do something nice for his mother because he was proud of her cooking skills.

He wasn't doing it out of guilt.

Fuck!

"So…"

Justin stopped dead in his tracks when he heard the deep voice of the man he detested. Turning, he saw Wes sauntering across the street towards him. Just what he didn't fucking need.

"I hear you're starting up a new business here in Passion. Aren't we Mr. High and Mighty Big Shot?"

"Get bent, Wes. I'm not in the mood."

Wes obviously didn't get the hint because he pursued. "Swinging into town with your fancy car and fancy clothes wasn't good enough, now you gotta show off by starting a restaurant for your mommy."

Just ignore him. Justin kept walking.

"Did mommy give you a big wet smoochie on your lips for that one? Bet it made you hot, didn't it? Maybe that's why you did it. You wanted your mommy to thank you in that 'special way'."

Justin spun on him, his fists ready when he saw the police cruiser pull to a stop at the curb. Wes was one lucky fucker.

"Problem?" Constable Millar asked while he stepped out of his car.

"Nope. Just out for a stroll, Constable." With a dirty wink in Justin's direction, he walked off.

"He giving you trouble? Tell me yes and I'll be happy to throw his sorry ass into jail."

"Nothing that warrants jail time. But I'll be sure to let you know if that changes."

"You do that. Hey, I heard about the restaurant you're putting up for your mamma. Good for you; it's about time she shared her goodies with the rest of us."

Smiling, Justin nodded. It was nice to finally have a voice of approval for what he was doing. "Thanks. And as soon as it opens, you bring your girl in for dinner. On the house."

"Can't wait. Take care, Justin."

"You, too." He watched the cruiser pulled away, then continued on his way to his mother's house. He found her outside, working in her flower beds.

"Hi, baby. Lovely day we're having, isn't it?"

He hadn't really noticed. "Do you have a minute?"

"For you, always." She wiped the sweat from her brow, then stood.

"You should be wearing a hat."

"It's not that hot out yet. I could use a nice, cold drink though. Care to join me?"

He nodded, then followed her into the house.

"What's up?"

"I just came from seeing Dad."

"That explains the sour look on your face."

He frowned. "No, that would be courtesy of Wes." He shook off her impending question. "Don't worry about it. Do you think the only reason I'm starting this restaurant for you is out of guilt from my past?" When she looked away, pouring two glasses of iced tea and said nothing, he had his answer. "Jesus, Mom."

"Are you?" She set a glass before him.

"No! I'm doing it because I think your skill deserves to be shared, because you have a gift, because you love to cook and bake. Pure and simple."

She nodded and took a chair across from him. "Okay."

"You don't believe me." God, that hurt.

"If what you say is true, then I believe you."

"Of course it's true. My God." Appalled, he stood, leaving his glass untouched. "Yes, okay, I feel guilty for the shit I put you through when I left, while I was gone, never calling or seeing you, but I'm not giving you this restaurant because of that. It never once entered my mind." He jumped when her hand touched his shoulder. He hadn't even heard her approach.

"Then I believe you."

"That's it? Now you believe me?"

"Yes I do." She stroked her hand along his cheek.

"Why? Because I rambled?"

Laughing, she held her hand to his cheek just a bit longer. "No, because your eyes never lie, and right now I see sincerity in them."

He let out a long breath, relaxing. "Now if only Dad had been that easy to persuade."

"He'll come around."

Justin shrugged. "So, do you wanna see where your restaurant is going to be built?"

"I would love to." Hooking her arm through Justin's, she followed him out.

Chapter Eighteen

Justin felt so much better now that he'd straightened things out with his mother. She loved the location for the restaurant, right off the highway where anyone who passed by would see it and be tempted to stop for a meal. It really was a smart location. And in three weeks they would be breaking ground. Which meant he would have to be back here in three weeks time. He wasn't going to miss the ground breaking of his very first restaurant.

After dropping his mother off, Justin went back to the floral shop and bought a bouquet of six white roses. He figured white was the best choice to cheer a person up, and he wanted Beth to have something to help her ease her mind. He couldn't imagine what it had been like for her, witnessing that child kill his father. Was it any wonder she'd come apart when she'd come home?

The sun was beginning to set as Justin pulled into her driveway. Since her car was parked in the driveway, he deduced that she was indeed home. If she hadn't been, he would have waited outside until she returned. Justin grabbed the bundle of roses on the passenger's seat and headed to her door. He rang the bell and waited for her to answer.

When the door opened, he broke out in a wide smile, only to have her slam the door in his face. "What the hell?" Yanking it open, he walked through the door only to receive one hell of an icy glare from her.

"Are you dense? Why do you think I slammed the door in your face?"

"I have no fucking clue." But the look on her face definitely showed her anger.

"What gives you the right to talk about me to my superior?"

"Um…my dad?"

"Yes, your father. You had no right to tell him I wasn't capable of working."

"I never said that." So that was why she was pissed at him. He really wished she would wear a sign that said why she was mad at him and save him the trouble of trying to get it out of her. "I went in to ask what happened with you last night, and he told me you'd witnessed a kid kill his father. Why didn't you tell me?"

"I didn't want to talk about it. He said you told him I broke down."

He blew out a breath; her anger was really draining him. "Yes, that I did say."

"You had no right."

"I was worried about you. God, Beth, you crumbled last night. I knew it had to be big."

"It was my business, not yours. Now I'm on desk duty until I talk to a goddamn shrink."

"Friends help friends when they're in need. I'm glad I was here when you got home. I'm glad I was able to ease the pain you must have been feeling, but you can't blame me for you having to see a shrink because, frankly, I think it's a good idea."

"I'm fine. I don't need a shrink." Throwing her arms in the air, Beth stormed off to her kitchen.

Justin followed her, the roses still in his hand. "Then you've got a serious case of denial, sweetheart."

"I'm not in denial. I dealt with it and now I'm fine."

Justin watched her pulled a beer from the fridge, pop the top, and guzzle nearly half down before pulling it from her lips. Oh yeah, she was dealing with it just fine. Since he didn't know what else to say to her, he simply held out the bouquet and smiled. "Maybe these will help."

She looked down at the roses and her eyes shimmered with tears.

"Jesus, they were supposed to cheer you up, not make you cry. I'll stop buying you flowers. Man." He felt like a complete louse now.

She sniffled, then reached out to take the flowers. "I love them, thank you. And I love the ones you planted outside." Then she slugged his arm good and hard, making him wince.

"What the hell was that for?" Jesus she had a nasty right jab.

"For filling my veranda with flowers."

She really knew how to spin his head. "I thought you just said you liked them."

"I do like them, but what gives you the right to plaster my place in flowers?" She set the roses in a vase with water.

"I was being nice. I thought if I showed you how much I care about you, then you'd finally give in to me." His lips slowly curled up with a sly smile. "It worked, more or less." She looked away and he could have sworn her cheeks had been red before she gave him her back. "Are you blushing?"

"It's time you left."

"I don't think so." He grabbed her arm when she tried to get past him, and though she shot him a killer look, he didn't release her. "You are blushing."

"Let me go, Justin."

"Not until you tell me why you're blushing." She looked so cute trying to look angry when her cheeks were still flushed with embarrassment.

"I wasn't thinking with my head last night." She finally blurted out.

"And thank your for that." He grinned wide.

Her eyes narrowed. "It never should have happened, and trust me, it won't happen again."

"The hell it won't."

She jerked her arm free and gave him a level glare. "Trust me, that was the first and only time."

"Trust *me*, that was only the beginning." He grabbed her around the waist and yanked her against his chest.

She laughed at him. "In your dreams."

"I bet if I were to touch you right now you would beg me for more." He tightened his grip when she tried to squirm out of his grasp.

She laughed again, a haughty, not-on-your-life sort of laugh. "You are so full of yourself."

"We'll see." In one quick motion, he cupped her between the legs and felt the heat she radiated warm his palm. "Oh yeah, you don't want me at all."

"Stop it." Her voice was anything but demanding.

"You and I both know you don't really mean that." He rubbed between her legs with his hand, sliding it up and down, feeling her arousal as it moistened her jeans.

"Yes…God, please…don't." Her eyes closed on her plea.

He kissed her passionately while he pushed her back, his hand still working her up. Her hands lifted now, to his arms and her fingers curled around his biceps and squeezed. She wanted him and there was no denying it now.

She began to gyrating, against his hand, and he would bet his precious car that if he continued stroking her, she would come in five seconds flat. He didn't want her feeling relief just yet. Pulling his hand away, her moan of protest vibrated against his lips sending a cascade of electrical charges throughout his body. Grabbing hold of her shirt with both hands, he tore it open at the front. She gasped, her short nails digging into his arms and her kisses growing more intense.

He spun her around, pressed her chest against the wall and then pressed himself into her. His genitals throbbed as he pinned her waist to the wall with his hips. "You want me, Beth. Admit it," he whispered against her ear and took great pleasure in the whimper that escaped her lips.

"I don't," she moaned, her body shaking.

"You do. Admit it." With both hands, he reached around her waist, then yanked the front of her jeans open with one hard jerk that sent the button bouncing off the wall to land at their feet.

"No," she panted, her hips pumping now.

"Say yes, Beth." He demanded against her ear. He didn't know why he was doing this to her. He'd never been forceful with any of his other sexual partners. But with Beth, well, it aroused him when she resisted him. *You are a sick one.*

"Say it, Beth," he insisted, yanking her jeans down in one hard pull.

She gasped, her breathing quickening. "Oh, God!"

"Tell me you want me, Beth." He shoved on hand into her panties, cupping her, while the other one slid up and took one breast. "Say it."

"I want you," she admitted in a burst.

"What do you want, Beth?" He teased her clit, making her squirm. She was so wet, so ready.

"You, now!" she panted, her hand clawing at the wall while her body bucked against his hand.

"Say my name when you tell me what you want." His fingers pinched her nipple and she gasped.

"I want you, Justin. Now!" She screamed it He spun her around, yanked her panties off then drew his zipper down. Grabbing one leg, he held it up, then plunged.

She cried out, and he felt her convulse around him, sucking him in, stroking his shaft in a wet slippery motion that nearly made his eyes cross. He slammed her good and hard against the wall, tore her bra aside then dove into all that tempting flesh. Her nipples were so hard, and when he grazed one with his teeth, she pumped him harder. She was wild, a bucking bronco, and he was more than happy to ride her until she broke.

He suckled, nibbled, and teased her breasts while he pumped himself into her. And when she convulsed around him again, he lost all control. With one final thrust, he poured himself into her.

His legs weak, he slid, with her against him, onto the floor.

"Damn," he laughed, feeling a euphoria he'd never felt before. He didn't think anything of it when she stood up. Until she spoke.

"I'm going to shower. Show yourself out."

He sat there a moment, trying to grasp what she'd just said. Then he stood, yanked his pants up and stomped up the stairs after her. He threw the bathroom door open, catching her off guard.

"Get out!"

"You are not doing this again. I'll admit I pushed you to do that, but you were a willing participant."

"I was willing, so don't go getting all panicky that I'll cry rape. Now get out," she insisted, grabbing a towel to cover her nudity.

"Fuck that. What the hell is going on with you, Beth?"

"Nothing is going on with me. Now, if you don't mind. I would like to take my shower. Alone."

"Feel free to shower, but I'm not leaving this time." He crossed his arms over his chest and leaned against the door, waiting.

"Really? So you've decided to move back to Passion then?"

"What? No, that wasn't what I meant."

"I didn't think so. Bye now." She stepped into the shower, pulled the curtain closed.

He yanked it open as she was bent over, hands on the faucets. "Is that what this is about, me not living here?"

"I really would like to take my shower now," she stated snidely.

"Answer the fucking question," he shouted at her.

"Yes!" she shouted back.

He stepped back, drew in a breath then spoke. "Okay, am I understanding this correctly. You don't want a relationship with me because I don't live here?"

"Yes."

"That's stupid."

Her blue eyes narrowed. "Go away now, Justin."

"What's wrong with a long distance relationship? And besides, I'm going to be here a hell of a lot for the next while. You'll see so much of me, you'll be eager to see me go."

She shook her head then started the water running. "Long distance relationships never work out."

"So you're just going to give up without trying?"

"Yes."

"But it was okay to have sex with me?"

She sighed. "Like I said, it never should have happened. End of discussion, Justin." She yanked the curtain shut again.

He blew out a long breath, then turning, stormed from the room.

That was just fucking bullshit.

~

Justin showed up at Tyler's door at just after ten. When his friend let him in, holding his finger to his lip, Justin figured either his wife or his son was already in bed. When Tyler informed him it was both, he was a little bit relieved. He wanted some time alone with his friend. Not that he didn't like Tyler's wife Lissy, he did, but what he wanted to discuss was more of a guy thing. And having his son awake would have distracted Tyler. Justin needed his full attention.

"What's up?"

"Your sister. What the hell is with her?" He threw out his hands in the air.

"Where do I start?" Tyler joked, taking a seat in the chair in his living room.

Justin was too restless to sit. "Okay, before I start, I have to know one thing. Would you deck me if I said I was sleeping with Beth?"

Tyler rubbed his hands on his trousers. "It doesn't look good for a loans officer to have battered knuckles.

So you're safe. For now," he warned.

"Okay, good. We've had sex, twice. First time she jumps me, and lord, she was an animal." Justin stopped when Tyler held his hand up.

"Please, do not go into detail because that will give me reason to deck you. I can always wear gloves."

"Fine, we'll leave it at her being an animal. In the morning, she all but thanks me for the lay and kicks me out. She had some issues at work and let's just say she used me to work it out of her system. Then today, well, crazy sex ensued once more. We're barely done and she boots me out the door."

"I don't know if I want to hear any more of this."

"You have to listen, man, I need some serious advice."

"About what? If it's sex with my sister, not going to happen, buddy."

"No, not sex. I can manage that myself." Justin finally sat. "What the hell do I do with her?"

Tyler leaned back, ran a hand across his face before responding. "She tell you why she keeps booting you to the curb?"

"Yeah, some shit about not wanting a long distance relationship, which is bull in my opinion."

"Why do you say that?"

"Lots of people have long distance relationships and they handle them just fine."

"Sure, but maybe those people haven't been hurt by the one they love."

"How have I hurt Beth?"

Tyler shook his head. "You didn't hear what I just said, did you?"

"I heard you just fine."

"Then what did I say?"

"You said maybe those people hadn't been hurt by the one they love." He held his hands out and shrugged.

Tyler shook his head again. "Beth loves you, Justin."

"Yeah, sure, and I love her, too." He snorted. What

was the biggie? He'd known her all his life. Sure he loved her, just like he loved his parents, his sisters, grandparents and so on.

"No, I don't mean love. I mean she is *in* love with you."

Justin snorted again, shaking his head. "Sure she is. Then why the hell does she keep pushing me away?"

"Because, she doesn't want to be hurt by you again."

"How the hell did I hurt her?" He was clueless.

"Jesus, Justin. You ran away. You didn't call her. You didn't write. For six years. Then you show up in town, make with the nice nice and get her hopes up, only to be hurt again when you leave town without saying goodbye to her."

"I tried to, but she was on patrol."

"You couldn't have told her the night before? To her, it felt like history repeating itself. She's been head over heels in love with you since—Christ—maybe always. When you left the first time, she was devastated. When you left this last time, well, she kinda broke. You can only have your heart smashed so many times before you put a guard up around it."

Justin couldn't believe what he was hearing. And he had no clue what to think about it. "Did she tell you all of this?"

"Nah, she told Lissy, who of course, told me. We have no secrets."

Justin's left eyebrow arced. "Does that mean this entire conversation will be relayed back to her?"

"You bet." Tyler grinned foolishly.

"Shit."

"It's no biggie; she won't say anything to anyone about it."

"She's in love with me?" Justin said softly, looking off at nothing in particular.

"My wife is not in love with you," Tyler teased.

"Why didn't I know about this? Why didn't I see it?" Justin continued, Tyler's humor gone to waste.

"Sometimes people are blind to what's right in front of them because it's not in their scope of reality. You thought of Beth as a friend, nothing more. Tell me something. What changed that now?"

"Have you looked at her?" Justin chortled.

"So it's a physical attraction?"

Lifting his foot, he rested it on the knee of his other leg. "If you're asking do I only want to have sex with her, then no. I find her incredibly attractive, sure, but there's more. I enjoy being with her, I enjoy conversations with her, hell, I even like fighting with her. None of that's changed."

"No, not that at least, but now you've got a physical attraction added into it. What do you want from this relationship?"

Tyler had always been good with the advice and easy to talk to. Now was no exception. But Justin wasn't sure he knew how to answer that. "Guess that's something I need to think about."

"Guess it is. She doesn't want to be hurt by you again, Justin. She'd much rather push you away than have her heart broken by you pushing her away. Love is not an easy thing to deal with. Trust me, I know this well." Tyler smiled like a man in love.

"Thanks, bro." Justin stood; their conversation swirling inside his mind giving him a headache. He was more confused now than he'd been before he came to his friend for help.

"Justin," Tyler called out and stopped him before Justin got to the door. "Take care with my sister, or you'll have to answer to me."

Nodding, understanding the warning, Justin left.

Beth was in love with him. Jesus, he just couldn't get past that. How could he have not known? Surely there had been signs. He ran over his past with Beth while he drove back to his hotel.

They'd spent so much time together before he'd left—well, when he wasn't hanging with Wes. They'd played basketball together, had water fights on hot summer nights, spent nights staring up at the stars, dreaming about what they would do when they were older. Beth had always been there when he'd needed help in school, tutoring him in math or helping him with a book report. Sitting with him when he'd been sick or talking with him when he'd had a run in with his father.

And so often she would look at him with that soft look, and she'd always glanced away the instant he'd looked back at her. Damn it! There were signs; he'd just been too damn blind to see them.

He pulled into his parking stall, climbed from his rental car, making sure to lock it up, then headed to his room. As he reached out to slide his key card into the slot, he noticed the door was ajar. Cocking his head to the side, he gave it a shove and with the light of the street lamp shining into the room, he saw the destruction.

Chapter Nineteen

He was absolutely stunned. The room was in a shambles, furniture tipped over, smashed, his clothing strewn around the room, the bedding ripped apart. And there was a strange stench in the air.

He flicked on the light and gasped.

On the wall, painted in what looked like the same red paint that had been used on his car, was a warning. *If you know what's good for you, LEAVE.*

Stepping over a broken chair, Justin walked into his room. The smell grew stronger, then he saw the pile of his clothing, and shook with rage. There, on some of his shirts, was a pile of excrement.

His head burnt with rage, his chest ached with it.

Turning away, Justin whipped his cell phone from his pocket and called his father. "I have a problem," he stated the instant it was answered. "Someone destroyed my hotel room. Yeah, I know, I'll wait outside." Tucking the phone back in his pocket, Justin walked from his room and sat on the hood of his rental car.

He sat, staring at the open door of his room, his vision clouded red.

Justin knew damn well who it was who had destroyed his room, and the bastard was not going to get away with it.

When he heard a car pull up behind him, he slid from his car, looking over just as his father exited his car.

"Have you been inside?" his father inquired.

"Yes."

"Touch anything?"

"I pushed the door open but that's it. You might want to plug your nose before you enter."

With a baffled look, he entered the room. Justin waited by his car while his father examined the destruction. He could only imagine what was going on inside of his father's head when he found the pile of dung.

It was a warm evening, but there was a chill in Justin's bones.

"I'm going to call in my team and have them go over the room." Vic stated the instant he exited the room.

"I know who did it."

"We're going to do this by the books, Justin. Speculation on who you think might have done this isn't enough to bring him in."

"Fine. I'll just go smash his fucking head in, then."

"You'll do no such thing. You do that and you give him the upper hand. Trust me on this, Justin. We'll get him, but we need to do this my way."

Justin nodded, though he still wanted to bust Wes' face in.

"Let's go to my office, and you can tell give me a statement."

Still fuelled by rage, Justin agreed. He waited while his father called in his team, glaring into his room. Justice was fine, but right now he wanted more.

"They'll be by shortly."

"Why is he doing this to me? I mean, I had nothing to do with him after I left. Any shit he got into was his own doing."

His father pulled out a cigarette and lit it, the flame lighting up a face that had been clouded by the darkness surrounding them. "Animosity. Resentment. You made something of yourself after you left. He's still here, working as a grease monkey with a rap sheet as long as my arm."

"Yeah. Shit, if I hadn't left I probably would be just like him." Justin shook his head and needed to pace off his anger. "No, I don't think that's true. I wanted to get away from him before I left because I knew he was only going to drag me down. That's why I walked away when he broke into the Gas 'N Gulp. He threatened me then, too. Damn." He wished now he had never befriended Wes.

"How did he threaten you?" his father asked calmly.

"He told me he'd beat my head in if I didn't help him. Jesus, I never thought he was seriously going to do it. It was talk; I thought it was talk. You know, *I'm big and tough; I could break into that store and steal everything in it and no one would ever fucking know.* We planned it out, how we would do it, yet still I didn't think he was serious. I sure as hell wasn't."

He paced and continued to ramble. "I thought we were going to drive around, grab some beer and…I don't know, just hang. But Wes stopped behind the store and got out, grabbing a bag from the backseat. God, I was so naive." He kicked a clump of rocks on the ground while he spoke. "It all sort of sunk in when he knelt down and pulled out the picks. He was seriously going to break in and rob the place. I couldn't do it, so I left. That's when he threatened me. Shit, I was such an idiot."

"You walked away. That's all that matters."

Justin looked at his father with utter astonishment.

"We'll get him for this, son."

The rage he'd been feeling before floated away like a feather and was replaced with a burning emotion he thought he'd never feel. His father believed him. God, when had been the last time he'd been called son? "You believe me?"

He nodded, dropping his cigarette on the ground and stomping it out. "You've had a clean record since leaving town six years ago. You made something of yourself, which I don't mind admitting now that I am damn proud of. You got into a lot of shit in your youth, but most of it was mild. Embarrassing as hell, sure, but they were misdemeanors. I've gone back over that night in my mind plenty of times since you came back, and…I believe you were not part of the break and enter."

The emotion not only burnt in his chest now, but in his eyes. For so long he'd been waiting to hear those words from his father. Now that he had, he was at a loss for words. "I…I don't know what to say."

"Say you'll forgive me for not believing in you."

God, his father was asking *him* for forgiveness. "You had reason to not believe me. I put you and Mom through hell with my rebellion. If anyone needs forgiveness, it's me."

His father held out his hand. "Then let's put an end to it here and now and start over."

The lump in his throat felt like a boulder when he tried to swallow. He took the first step, then the second, moving slowly towards his father. With his heart on his sleeve, he took his father's hand. And was completely shocked when he was pulled towards his father, then engulfed by his strong arms.

His eyes burnt with tears of love.

He was released when the cars approached, and Justin did his best to hide his tears. But when his father turned his head to the vehicles approaching, Justin saw the shimmer of dampness on his father's cheeks.

~

Drinking her morning cup of coffee and admiring the beautiful day, Beth sulked. She'd called in sick, which was an anomaly for her. She never called in sick, even when she *was* sick. But damn it, she was pissed off that she'd been put on desk duty. Like she was so fucking unstable that she couldn't be trusted out in the field. Like she'd go ballistic on some poor speeder on the highway and blow his head off. She snorted. That was so not in her character. Sure, the shooting had upset her, and yes, she had crumbled, but she'd gotten it out of her system. For the most part.

The nightmares were problematic, but she could deal with them. She could deal with the look on the poor boy's face when he'd confessed his need to kill his father before his father killed them. She could deal with his misery and the sad look on his face as he was taken away from his mother.

It was that look that haunted her in her sleep.

Leaving her coffee on the table, Beth pushed from her seat and wandered the large veranda. Okay, so maybe she did need to talk to the shrink. But she wasn't that unstable that she was a risk on the job.

The scent of flowers warmed by the sun caught her attention. There wasn't a section of the ledge that surrounded the veranda that wasn't hanging with a planter. Justin had gone all out in his attempt to win her over. She loved the colors, bright red and virginal white.

Breaking off a carnation, Beth held it to her nose and breathed in the fragrant scent. It reminded her of Justin, the way he'd smelled when she'd collapsed in his arms. When she'd thrown herself at him and demanded to be taken.

God, what had gotten into her? She'd been so forceful, so demanding, so…animalistic. She'd thought it had simply been her emotional state at the time, but she'd been just as wild when he'd taken her against the wall. He brought the animal out in her, and she wasn't sure how to deal with that.

She'd never been that wild before.

What was she going to do about him? She sighed, clutching the flower to her breast. She loved him with all her heart and soul, but she knew she was destined to be without him. He wasn't going to move back to Passion simply for her. He had a new life, a better life than he could ever have here. She had nothing to offer him. Passion was her home; she never planned on leaving it.

Well, unless she was transferred somewhere because of her job. She'd hate to have to leave, but she loved her job and she'd go wherever it took her.

She loved Justin more than she loved anything else, yet she was pushing him away. Only because she didn't want her heart continually broken. Yet being without him was killing her. She wanted to be in his arms, she wanted to feel his hands on her body, his mouth on her lips. She wanted to sit on the veranda in the morning and enjoy her first cup of coffee surrounded by the plethora of flowers he'd surrounded her in.

Being without him was killing her. Maybe it was time to give in and take what she could get from him. It might work out; then again, it might not. But at least she could take solace in knowing she'd had him for a time. However long it might be.

When she saw his car pull up the road that led to her property, her heart sped up and her stomach tied in knots. As he stepped from the car and the sun lit his blond hair with streams of gold, she let herself go.

No more resisting, Beth, it's time to live a little.

"Now that is a beautiful site to behold."

She practically ran to him, but she couldn't stop herself. Throwing her arms around his neck, she kissed him with a hard, desperate kiss she knew did more than shock him. She could feel his reaction as it jabbed her in her belly.

"Whoa. I wasn't expecting that." He laughed when she pulled herself away.

"I'm tired of fighting myself. I'm tired of thinking of reasons why we shouldn't be together. I want you, Justin, for how ever long I can have you." And she wanted him now. With a quick jump, she wound her legs around his waist and devoured his lips. She didn't care where they were or who saw them, she needed him, here and now.

"Whoa, slow down there."

"No, I want you, now."

He took hold of the hand she was currently using to

rip his shirt open, and pressed it to his lips. "Then you can have me. But not here, not like this."

She wasn't sure what to expect when he carried her to the house. Her body was on fire with need and if it wasn't sated soon she might just scream. When he set her on the bed, she began removing her clothing in a mad rush.

"Slow down," he told her, placing his hands over hers. "Let me."

She swallowed the lump in her throat then when he knelt before her, and drew her jeans down. He took his time, slowly slipping them past her waist, over her hips and down her legs. And when he pulled them free, he kissed his way up her left leg, nibbling on the back of her knee which sent a chill of erotic pleasure throughout her body.

He was so tender, so caring that it brought tears to her eyes. As she lay back on the bed, he kissed his way down her right leg. When he bit her big toe, she gasped and felt herself moisten. Pain was suddenly a turn on for her. *Now, wasn't that bizarre?*

His hands skimmed up the sides of her legs and she quivered. When he took hold of her hands and pulled her up, she prepared for the kiss. God, she craved the kiss. Instead, he took the hem of her shirt, and slowly slid it up her body, over her head. Then with a smoldering look of desire in his eyes, he unhooked her bra.

Her breasts fell free only to be cupped by his hands. She kept her eyes on his while he massaged them, gently, erotically. She felt like she couldn't breathe though she knew she was panting.

"I want to savor you," he said, then pressed her down onto the bed.

His hands roamed her body, touching everywhere, teasing, tormenting, caressing. He rubbed his palms over her nipples, making them harden even more. His mouth sampled the skin behind her ears and along her chin. Using his teeth, he nipped her neck, and the sensation speared right into her belly.

"God, yes," she panted, tilting her head back to allow him easier access. She wanted more. He didn't disappoint.

With torturously slow motion, he pulled her panties away. The air chilled the dampness between her legs, but it was a welcome breeze over the blaze that had erupted over her body. She spread for him, expecting him to take her now, then gasped when his mouth engulfed the heat. He used his tongue in the most wicked way, flicking, sliding, licking, probing. He drove her to insanity with his mouth, but it was when he used his teeth that sent her right over the edge.

She bucked, her back arching, her hands clawing at the bedding beneath her. She felt lost in the sensations exploding inside of her and crazy to have it all.

He gave her that and more.

Her body still twitching and begging for more was disappointed when he stopped. But when he slid that wicked mouth along her belly and all the way up to her mouth, she knew it was anything but over.

Thank God!

He stood up and stripped from his clothing. "I'm going to make love to you now, nice and slow," he promised, then slipped inside of her.

Her back arched as he entered her, and she couldn't wait for the pounding he was sure to give her. Only this time, he took her mouth and barely moved inside of her. He kissed her with such sensuality it took her breath away. With his hands braced on either side of her head, he moved inside of her with one slow stroke after another.

His tongue seduced hers while his body took her on a ride she'd never had before.

There was love in each stroke he made inside of her. If he never said he loved her, at least she would forever have this.

"Look at me, Beth."

She opened her eyes, and looking into the deep,

blue ocean of his gaze upon her, she let herself go.

The orgasm came on slow and seemed to last forever. She never once took her eyes off of his, even when his own release erupted inside of her.

~

Moments later, while Beth lay in his arms, nestled against his chest, Justin thought about what she'd said before she'd jumped him. "What changed your mind?"

"Hm," she sighed, snuggling a little closer.

"What changed your mind? Why suddenly are you okay with us?"

She shifted against him before speaking. "I want to be with you. If that's for a week, then I'll cherish that week."

"You know, I never knew you to be such a skeptic." He tilted her head so he could look her in the face. "I told you, I'll be back here often while the restaurant is being built, and after that, I'll be hiring staff and getting it ready to open. We'll see plenty of each other."

"Sure."

"You could take some time off and come stay with me for a week." He wanted very much to show her what he'd accomplished after he'd left.

After he left. His conversation with Tyler shot into his mind.

She was in love with him. He'd devastated her when he'd left, both times.

He wasn't ready to deal with the love aspect yet, but he could discuss the other stuff. Sitting up, he looked down at her as he spoke. Seemed to be an evening for him pouring his heart out. "I'm sorry I left without telling you, without saying goodbye."

"Which time?" she asked, plumping her pillow and sitting up.

"Both. I should have called you the first time, even if just to say goodbye. It was selfish of me. You deserved more. If it's any consolation, I missed you like crazy."

She shrugged nonchalantly. "A little."

"I was scared, bitter, and felt like everyone was against me. But I should have known better than to think that about you. You've always been there for me, always been my best friend, and I'm sorry for hurting you." The sunlight shining through her bedroom window illuminated the tears glistening in her eyes.

"And this last time?"

With his thumb he wiped the tear sliding down her cheeks. "I wanted to, but that's not good enough. I should have told you the night before."

"When you snuck into my room?" She smiled faintly.

"Yeah. Don't cry, okay. I really am sorry." He kissed her quivering lips while his hands cupped her face.

They made love for most of the morning, and when she finally fell asleep in his arms near noon, he kissed her head, then closed his eyes.

He knew he loved her, always had, always would.

But would it be enough for her if he couldn't love her in the same way she loved him?

Chapter Twenty

Beth woke to the rhythmic jingle of a cell phone. Sitting up, she rubbed her tired eyes and tried to make out where it was coming from. Following the sound, she climbed over the bed, careful not to step on Justin's legs, and found the source of the sound. It was coming from Justin's pants. Grabbing them, she pulled the cell phone from his pocket.

Glancing at the I.D, she recognized Vic's office number.

"What are you doing?"

She squealed, dropping the cell phone.

Laughing, Justin sat up. "Sorry."

"Jerk." Reaching down, she picked up the phone and thrust it out to him. "Your phone was ringing."

He took it and set it beside him on the bed. "If it's important, they'll leave a message. Damn, you're sexy. Come here, gorgeous."

He yanked her down on top of him and grabbed her ass. She felt him hard and ready, pressing against her. More than ready to accommodate him, she pulled her legs up, bending at the knees, then sat up over him.

Then her phone rang.

"Let it go."

She wanted to. His hands were busy working her into a frenzy, but she hated a ringing phone. "Just let me see who it is and get rid of them." She scooped the phone up, trying to concentrate on the call and not

Justin's busy hands. "Hello."

"Beth. Is Justin there? I've tried his cell and the hotel and thought I'd take a chance and see if he was with you."

She slapped Justin's hands away and climbed off of him. "Yes, Vic, he's here." Beth held the phone out to Justin, and she was pretty sure her face was beat red.

He took the phone and while he spoke, she grabbed her robe and slipped it on.

"What do you mean you have nothing to arrest him on? What about prints? Witnesses? Damn it! Yeah, yeah, I know. I won't. I won't," he emphasized angrily. "Yeah, I'll go talk to the manager and see if they can get me into another room. I'll talk to you later."

He was angry, but Beth had no idea why. "What's up?"

"Fucking Wes. I am going to kill him."

"Whoa, don't be making those kinds of threats around me. What did he do now?"

"He trashed my room, wrote a threatening message on the wall in red paint, and shit on my clothes. And he's going to fucking get away with it. Bastard." He threw the covers back and jumped out of bed.

"He did that in broad daylight?" She belted her robe, giving Justin her full attention.

"No. Last night. Had to have been between the time I left here and went to Tyler's," he explained, running a hand across his face.

"Last night? Why didn't you tell me that when you got here this morning?" It hurt that he hadn't told her about it.

"You, uh, didn't give me time to say much." He sent her a sly smile.

She cleared her throat. He was right, she hadn't. "Oh, right."

"My father just informed me that there were no witnesses, no one saw anything unusual, no one saw him break into my hotel room, and there's nothing concrete in the room to place him as the culprit."

"He defecated on your clothes?"

Justin yanked on his pants. "Yeah, a nice healthy dump. I got the message loud and clear. It's what he thinks of me and the fact that I made something of myself when he didn't."

"What was the threat?"

Justin shook his head. "It doesn't matter."

"Yes, it does," she insisted. "What did it say?"

"Look at you, all protective." He growled it while he stalked his way towards her.

"What did it say, Justin?" She stepped back because she knew if he touched her, she wouldn't want him to stop.

"'If you know what's good for you, leave.' Big, bold, and red. It looked like the same red that was used on my car. Now come here and take my mind off my troubles."

He yanked her towards him, then swept her off her feet and carried her to the bed.

~

After four hours of vigorous lovemaking, Justin left her bed with the promise to be back for dinner and round two. Beth refused his demand that she be naked in bed when he returned, explaining she had an appointment to keep. It had been a lie, but she knew if she told him what she really had planned, he wouldn't have let her.

After a quick shower, Beth hurried out the door and headed to work. She pulled up to the building just as Vic did.

"I thought you were sick?" Vic mocked sarcastically, exiting the car.

"I lied. I was pissed off about having to see the shrink," she admitted freely.

"I figured as much. Figured it had to be something major for you to call in sick. I'm not changing my mind, if that's why you're here."

"It's not. I'll go see the shrink," Beth said with a

roll of her eyes. "I came in to talk to you about the incident in Justin's room last night."

"He told you about it, I take it?" Vic held the door for her as they entered the depot.

"Yeah, but he didn't go into a lot of details."

"Any messages, Millie?"

"Your wife called. Said she'd be late tonight. She got a call from Miss Heather. She hurt her hip and asked Julia to come by and cook her a few meals that she can pop in the microwave."

"That's my girl. Always the humanitarian."

"Hey, Millie."

"Beth. You feeling better now?"

Beth grinned slyly. So everyone knew her supposed illness had been bullshit. "Yes, thank you." She followed Vic into his office and took a seat while he booted up his computer.

"Here are the shots from the room." Shifting his monitor, Vic lit a cigarette while Beth looked at the scene.

She read the threat, her hands bunching on her lap, and when she saw the close-up of the excrement on his clothing, she was spitting mad. "Jesus. You send any of that in for analysis?" They were nice clothes, too. Justin had such nice taste, and to have someone ruin them in such a way was horrible.

Vic blew out a stream of smoke then spoke. "You know the drill. It goes on the list according to priority. Murder always comes before B and E."

Beth nodded, still furious. "Any prints?"

"Several. Same deal. No one saw or heard anything, so essentially, I have nothing."

"Great. So he gets away with it, again."

"We don't know who is responsible."

Beth gave him a get-real sort of look.

"We have no proof. Yes, I believe Wes is the one responsible for the vandalism and B and E, but without proof, we can't pursue it."

"This bites." She stood, shoving her hands in her

jeans' pockets. "Why can't he just let it go? Get over it? Leave Justin alone?"

"Because he resents the fact that Justin did something with his life after he left. At least that's my take on it. Wes has never been all there upstairs, if you know what I mean. His father smacked him around quite a bit in his youth."

"And that gives him the right to do what he's doing?"

"No, I'm just giving you a look at where he came from. I'm doing all I can to try and get him for this. But until we have something concrete…well, he gets off."

The hell with that, Beth thought later as she climbed into her car. Wes Donnelly was not getting away with it. Not if she had her way. She pulled up to the curb in front of Wes' house, determined to make him confess.

She rang the bell and waited. When he finally answered, still dressed in his greasy coveralls, she deduced he'd just returned home from work.

"What do you want?" Wes snarled.

"Can I come in and talk?" *Be polite. You won't get anywhere being nasty.*

"You wanna come in and talk to me?" Was asked with surprise.

"Yes, please." It was killing her to have to fake joviality, but it would be worth it, in the end. She hoped.

He stepped aside, his mouth curving in a smile that made Beth shudder inside. "Well, since you asked so nicely."

"Thank you. Did I get you away from anything?" She stepped into his house and wasn't surprised by what she saw. It was a filthy mess, newspapers strewn on the floor and the furniture. Beer bottles sitting on the coffee and end tables, and it smelt of cigarettes and garbage.

"I just got home from work. Was gonna make

something to eat, but it can wait."

The way he said that gave her the creeps. If he thought she was here on a personal basis, he was about to get the surprise of his life. "I'll try not to keep you long, then." Pulling the newspaper from the battered gold tweed chair in his living room, Beth sat. She didn't want to be here long. "I'd like to talk to you about Justin."

"Shoulda known you weren't here for me." He sat on the sofa, grumbling his response. "I got nothing to say about him."

"You seemed to have a lot to say when you spray painted his car and hotel room, though." She watched him for any signs of guilt but he held his composure.

"Wasn't me who did it."

She was not going to give up. "You and I both know that's a lie. Why can't you leave him alone, Wes? He hasn't done anything to you."

Wes snorted. "He ruined my life."

"How did he ruin your life? He wasn't with you when you broke into the local store, and he wasn't there when you were arrested for all your other crimes."

"If he'd stayed with me at the Gas 'N Gulp like we agreed, I wouldn't have been arrested."

Her brow rose in surprise. "You broke into a business, Wes. What makes you think having Justin there would have prevented you from being arrested? You were caught breaking into the place."

"His daddy would have fixed it so we wouldn't have gotten into trouble for it."

She blinked in complete shock. "Are you for real? You think that if Justin had stayed, Vic would have let the two of you go?" She chuckled, which angered him. "You both would have been arrested. Vic wouldn't have let the two of you go. Even if Justin had been there. It's his job."

"He always managed to get his precious son out of his jams before."

"Those were misdemeanors. Vandalism, rowdiness, drunk and disorderly. Minor infractions compared to B and E."

Wes shrugged boney shoulders. "I'm betting Vic would have found some way around it."

She shook her head in disbelief. "So because of that, you're causing Justin trouble now. He's not responsible for your criminal past."

"The way I see it, he is."

Did he realize he more or less confessed to terrorizing Justin? "Leave him alone, Wes."

He laughed, tipping his head back. "This is funny. He's got a girl protecting him now. If it's not his daddy, it's his girl." He leaned forward, his eyes narrowed. "Why don't you give me a reason to?" He stood now and slunk his way towards her.

She didn't like that look in his eyes, and as she stood, she wished she'd brought her weapon. "I think it's time I left." When he grabbed her arm, her defenses came up. "Remove it, Wes."

"You want me to leave your precious Justin alone. Give me incentive." He spun her around and shoved her down onto the sofa. He was on top of her before she had a chance to react.

~

There hadn't been much he could salvage from his hotel room. He certainly wasn't taking the clothing Wes had soiled, even if they could be cleaned. The memory would be enough to stop him from ever wearing them again. He'd agreed with the hotel staff and his father had been okay with it, that Justin would clean up his soiled clothing. It wasn't the cleaning staff's responsibility, not that it was his either, but better him than some poor cleaning woman.

Besides, he was going to enjoy dumping the lot on Wes' front door after the guy went to bed tonight. Let him deal with his own shit.

It pissed him off that Wes was going to get away with it.

Again!

He was just about to climb behind the wheel of his rental car, when his mother pulled up. Justin tossed the garbage bag with his soiled clothing in the back seat, not wanting his mother to have to see it.

"Hey, what are you doing here?"

"This is the first chance I've had to get away. Oh, baby, I am so sorry for what happened to your room."

He wondered what all his father had told her. "Yeah, me, too."

"Did he leave you any clothing?"

"Just what I have on." Which he was going to remedy tomorrow when the local clothing store was open.

His mother shook her head, then touched his face. "Why don't you come stay with us instead of staying in…there." She pointed to the room, shaking her head again.

"I hadn't planned on staying in that room. I appreciate the offer, but I think I'll stay at Beth's for the next few days." Not that he'd asked her yet, but he was sure she wouldn't object.

Her brow lifted in amusement. "Oh,"

"You're probably going to find out sooner or later. Small town gossip, and all. Beth and I are a couple."

"I know. Small town gossip, and all." She smiled. "I was just waiting for my son to confirm. That's nice. About time Beth finally told you how she felt about you."

"You know that she…loves me?"

His mother laughed, touching his cheek again. "I don't think there's a person in town that doesn't know that."

"Well, I am an idiot." Apparently he was the only clueless person around.

"All's well that ends well."

"See, that's the thing. I don't know what to do about the way she feels towards me."

"Do you love her?"

"Sure," he said, running a hand through his hair. "But not the same way she loves me. I don't think." He paused. "I just don't know. Yes, I enjoy being with her, and we have great sex—conversations," he amended, reminding himself he was speaking to his mother.

Laughing, she rubbed her hand up and down his arm. "It's okay, baby. You're a big boy now, I know you have sex."

He was sure his face was red, but he continued, "The idea of being away from her, being without her...well, it makes my chest feel funny, but I don't know if it'll last."

"You're just beginning your relationship. Enjoy the moment and go with your heart." She leaned over and kissed his cheek. "It will always lead you in the right direction."

Chapter Twenty-one

He had her arms pinned to the sofa with his knees. Every training session she'd been in flashed through her head. Only problem was, fear clouded it.

Beth knew she was going to be raped, and she was clueless how to stop it.

"I'm gonna enjoy taking Justin's girl."

He tore her shirt down the center, and Beth screamed. She had that much knowledge in her to know to scream. But then he clamped his hand over her mouth, smothering her.

"Shut the fuck up!" he shouted at her, leaning in real close. Grabbing hold of the clasp on her jeans, he yanked it open. "You can scream all you like when I'm fucking you, but not until then."

You can't let this happen, Beth, come on, think. Teeth, use your teeth. She shook her head sharply which caused his hand to shift, and then she sunk in with her teeth.

"Jesus," he screamed, pulling his hand away and it was enough of a distraction that she was able to buck him off of her.

He fell backwards onto the sofa and Beth scrambled to her feet. When he lunged at her, she screamed and ran for the door. He caught up with her, grabbing her arm and Beth spun on him, fist ready. With a solid jab, she ploughed her fist into his nose. The only problem was, it didn't slow him down enough for her to make a break for it. The back of his hand came up fast and slashed across her mouth. She tasted blood, felt the room spin, but kept her head. Lifting her foot, she kicked him square in the nuts. He buckled, falling to the floor on his knees, and Beth yanked the door open and ran for her car.

Shoving the keys in the ignition, she set herself rolling, tires squealing. Her hands shook on the wheel, so she tightened her grip. Her legs began to quiver, and she told herself just to stay calm.

He hadn't raped her; she was safe and she had what she needed to put him away and stop Wes from tormenting Justin. She came to a halt at the front of the police depot and slamming from her car, Beth ran for the front door. She yanked it open and was startled to find Millie directly on the other side.

"Beth. Oh, my God! What happened?"

Her legs threatened to buckle, but she refused to allow them. "Wes…attacked me." Millie caught her as her knees gave out. Damn it, she was stronger than this.

"Sweet God. Vic, Vic, get in here. I need your help," Millie called out, helping Beth towards his office.

"I'm okay," Beth insisted, though the room was a little fuzzy.

"What are you…? Shit, what happened?" Vic ran to Beth, taking hold of her other side.

"Wes Donnelly attacked her," Millie stated.

Beth knew they were helping her to Vic's office, but she honestly couldn't feel her legs beneath her while she walked. "I'm okay."

"The hell you are. Get a cold cloth," Vic instructed Millie as they sat Beth down in the chair. Millie ran off, and Vic knelt down in front of Beth. "Did he rape you, Beth?"

She shook her head and it felt like jelly. "He tried but I stopped him. You have to arrest him. Now he'll leave Justin alone." Her eyes rolled to the back of her head and it all went black.

~

Justin flew into the local clinic like a whirlwind. His mind was solely focused on finding Beth and making sure she was alright. His father's phone call had been vague, stating that Beth had been injured and they were taking her to the clinic. He envisioned her being beaten up by a perp, possibly in a car accident or…and this is what scared him the most, shot.

His chest ached as he ran for the front desk. "Beth Healy. Where is she?"

"Justin."

He spun around to see his uncle and aunt along with his mother, sitting in the quiet waiting room. "Where is she? What happened?"

"Maybe you should sit down," His mother advised, taking him by the arm.

"Oh, Jesus, she was shot, wasn't she? Shit, how bad? Is she alive—oh, dear God, tell me she's alive." His chest suddenly felt like it might crack open.

"She's alive," his uncle reassured him. "She was attacked."

"What? By who? When? I need to see her. Where is she?"

"The doctor is checking her out now," Cassie explained with a quiver in her voice.

He didn't like this. They were hiding something. Then he heard his father's voice, and when he turned, he saw him walking with Beth, his arm around her.

Then it all faded when he caught sight of Beth's bruised, swollen lip.

He jumped up and ran to her. "How are you? Jesus, what happened? Who did this?"

"Slow down, Justin," his father advised.

"I'm okay." Beth tried to smile, but Justin could see that it was faked. "I just want to go home."

"Are you okay, sweetie?" Cassie asked, taking her daughter's hands.

"I am now. Nothing happened," she said in a reassuring tone.

"The hell nothing happened. Who beat you up?" Justin demanded.

"I want to go home," Beth said in a voice so light it nearly floated.

"We'll take you home, sweetie." Putting his arm around his daughter, Tom gave her a gentle squeeze.

"Will someone talk to me, please?"

"Not here," His father said in a low tone. "Why don't you come home with us, son, and I'll fill you in."

"I'm not leaving Beth." Pulling away, Justin hurried after her while she was led from the clinic. She was being tucked into her parents' car when Justin got outside. So he climbed into his car and followed. His mind was reeling, his chest was aching, and all he wanted was to hold Beth in his arms and make sure she was okay.

He pulled up behind his aunt and uncle, then hurried to the house. Beth let them in, and it was then that he noticed she wore his father's jacket.

"I'll help you to bed," Cassie said, still holding her daughter to her side.

Justin jumped in front of her, his eyes scanning her face. "Talk to me, Beth. What happened and why are you wearing my father's jacket."

"I…I'm okay, Justin," she said, touching her hand to his face.

The jacket split open in the front and Justin saw her torn shirt. "What the hell—" He yanked the jacket open and his eyes went wide. "Were you—"

"No!" She took a deep breath then replied calmly. "He tried, but I stopped him."

"Who? Who the hell did this to you?" he demanded.

"Wes."

Justin felt the color drain from his face.

"We need to get you to bed." Cassie took her daughter by the waist.

"I want a shower first," Beth informed her mother while she was led up the stairs.

"I'm going to kill that bastard." Justin spun around, ready to make good on his threat and was stopped by a wall of a man. "Move out of my way, Uncle Tom."

"As much as I want that bastard to pay for what he did to my little girl, I can't let you run off and do something stupid."

"He attacked her. Her clothes are torn, and he might very well have raped her."

"She told you he didn't."

"I know what she told me, but—"

"She wasn't raped," his father reassured him as he entered the house.

"How do you know?" Justin questioned his father.

"Her exam was negative. And she gave me the details. He tried, but she fought him off and got away."

The relief wrapped around his heart and eased the ache in his chest. "You'd better tell me you have him in custody."

Vic let out a long breath, then shook his head. "He wasn't at his house when my officers went to arrest him. We have an APB out on him. He won't get far, Justin."

"He damn well better not." Justin glanced up as Cassie came down the stairs. "How is she?"

"Shaken up. She's taking a shower. Did you get him?" she asked and received a head shake.

"I need to see her." Ignoring the protests, Justin rushed up the stairs. He threw the door open and cursed himself when Beth yelped. What was he thinking? "I'm sorry. I just needed to see you." She clutched the towel to her breast, and he could see her hands shaking. "God, Beth. I am so sorry." She went into his arms and her body shook while she cried.

He held her—he wasn't sure how long—and just let her cry. Inside, he was imagining all the things he could do to Wes to make him pay. When she sniffled and lifted her head, he cupped her face in his hands, then kissed her swollen lip with a gentle, loving kiss. "Better?"

She smiled at him and his heart felt relieved. "Much."

"How did it happen?"

"Justin—"

"I just need to know."

She sighed, grabbing a wad of tissue paper to blow her nose. "I went to him to ask him to leave you alone."

"What!" She jumped again, and he cursed to himself. "Sorry. Why would you do that?"

"Because I wanted him to leave you alone," she blurted out and the tears began to fall again.

"Okay, okay, I'm sorry I yelled. Shh, baby, come here." He took her into his arms and stroked her hair.

"I just thought I could trick him into admitting what he did to your car and your hotel room, and we could put him behind us."

He cupped her face again and shook his head. "My protector. My idiot." He thumped her head lightly with his fist. "You scared the hell out of me." He kissed her mouth gently. "Don't be my protector, okay."

"I just wanted him to leave you alone."

"I know. Shh now. Come on, let's get you in the shower. Are you bruised anywhere besides your mouth?"

She shook her head.

"Okay." That was a relief. He started the water, tested the temperature, then helped her under the spray. Then he disrobed.

"What are you doing?" she asked softly.

"Taking care of my girl." He stepped into the shower, closed the curtain, then picked up the soap. She let him wash her, and he sensed she knew his motive for it. He wanted to wash everything of Wes off of her and, in doing so, wanted her to remember his gentle hands touching her body. Not the greedy ones of his enemy.

Justin took his time washing her, scrubbing her hair, and reveling in the scent of her shampoo. "Please, let your hair grow out."

She laughed and it was music to his ears. “I don’t like it short, either.”

“Then why the hell did you cut it?”

Her chin lifted, a faint smile on her lips. “Because it reminded me of the way you ran your hands through the length.”

“You are a crazy woman,” he said with a smile, shaking his head. “No wonder I’m in love with you.” They both froze. Justin’s eyes met hers in wide bafflement. Where the hell had that come from?

“Please tell me you didn’t just say that because of what happened to me?”

“No, holy shit. No, I think I meant it.” He laughed. Then took her face in his hands and kissed her forehead. “I think I’m in love with you.”

“Well, guess what Justin? I know I’m in love with you.”

He held her in his arms while the water ran over them, washing her free of her ordeal.

~

At his insistence, Beth took a sleeping pill and curled up in bed. He lay with her in his arms while she drifted off to sleep. She’d been brave—and stupid—trying to protect him, but she was the one that needed the protection. Justin wanted to be her guard and make sure nothing bad ever happened to her again.

When he was sure she was fast asleep, he slid from her side, tucking her in before he tiptoed from her room. And was completely shocked to see everyone, including his mother and Beth’s brothers, waiting for him.

“Wow, full house.”

“How is she?” Cassie asked instantly.

“Asleep. I made her take a sleeping pill. She did this for me?” His eyes met his father’s and he received a nod of recognition. “Will this put him away?”

“For some time, yes. It’s his second assault,” Vic informed him.

“Good.” Suddenly feeling drained, Justin dropped

down onto the sofa.

"We've got not just our team and surrounding areas looking for him, but the city also. Wes won't get far," he reassured Justin with a hand on his shoulder.

"If he hasn't been caught by the time I have to fly out in two days, I'm taking her with me."

"Justin—"

"She's been through hell these past few days. She needs to get away."

"She's a cop; she's trained to deal with things differently," his father advised him.

"She's also a woman," Justin pointed out. "She was assaulted. All the cop training doesn't negate that fact. Does she have time coming that she can take?"

His father nodded.

"Then she's coming with me, not permanently, but for a vacation."

"She needs to see a counselor," Cassie pointed out.

Justin nodded. "I'll make sure she sees someone."

"It has to be departmental."

"Then find someone in Mississauga. I'm taking her away from this for a while, no arguments. Now, I need something to eat before I drop."

While his mother busied herself in Beth's kitchen, preparing Justin something to eat, both his uncle and aunt pulled him aside.

"She's going to argue with you that she's more than capable of dealing with this on her own."

"I'm stubborn, too," Justin pointed out.

Tom smiled. "Yeah, you two should have an interesting relationship. We'll help you convince her."

"We want her safe," Cassie stated, her eyes a little teary. "We know you'll make sure she is."

Later, when the house was empty and everyone had gone home, Justin sat in the living room in complete darkness. He was physically and mentally drained. There was food in his belly, thanks to his mother, but it wasn't sitting right.

His belly wouldn't feel right until Wes was put

behind bars.

Beth was still sound asleep in her bed, and that gave him some comfort. Dragging himself off the sofa, Justin headed for the stairs. He was going to curl up beside the woman he loved and make sure nothing ever hurt her again.

"I thought they'd never leave."

Justin turned, something hit his head and he went down.

Chapter Twenty-two

Pain erupted like a starburst before his eyes. Falling to the floor, Justin felt the meal his mother had made him rise with an acrid taste in his throat. Even in the darkness he knew the room was spinning.

He just couldn't make it stop.

"I had a feeling you'd be here. Which makes it all the more perfect."

That was Wes's voice, however muddled it sounded. He lost his breath and his side burst into flames of pain when a foot connected with his ribs. He rolled on the floor, coughing and sputtering. When a light came on, Justin slammed his eyes shut, his head despising the sudden brightness.

"You know, if you'd stayed away, everything would have been fine. But no, you had to come to town, Mr. Big Shot, showing off that you were a big man now."

The blow to his other side had the bile stinging his throat as the slash of pain speared into his ribs.

"Well, I showed you just who the man was, didn't I? Your sweetie tastes mighty fine." He knelt down and gripped Justin's face in his hands. "She felt even better. Nice tits, firm, ripe."

Justin threw his hands up, but it was a pathetic attempt. His vision was so wonky that he only flailed at the air.

Wes stood, laughing. "You are pathetic. No wonder she has to protect you. What does she see in you?

You're not a man. A real man would stand and fight for his woman. Well, maybe I need to go show her just what a real man is."

Through blurry eyes, Justin saw Wes walk towards the stairs. *Get up, you fool. Stop him.* Rolling onto his side, Justin got to his knees, fighting the nausea. He braced his hand on the couch, and pushed to his feet. "Stop," he called out, stumbling towards Wes.

"You're pathetic. I'm going to enjoy taking your woman."

The strength came to him out of nowhere and Justin lunged at Wes. His hands caught the bottom of his shirt and knocked him off balance. "Leave her alone," Justin growled at him, fighting back the nausea and pain. He lost his balance and took Wes down with him. They tumbled down the stairs, landing with a thud at the bottom.

"You don't have the strength to take me down," Wes laughed at Justin as he pushed to his feet.

"The hell I don't." Justin stood, wobbled but held his ground, then curled his fist and sucker punched Wes in the face.

They grappled, fists flying and stumbled into an end table, sending the lamp crashing to the floor.

~

Beth woke with a start. Sitting up in her bed, the room dark, she tried to focus. Her head was so foggy, and her eyes refused to stay open. The crash jolted her and her eyes shot open wide.

Someone was in her house. Someone was breaking in.

Listless and groggy, she slid from the bed, her robe floating behind her when she walked to her closet. There was another crash, and her heart began to pound.

She needed her gun. Where the hell was her gun? She should phone for help. But she needed her gun first. Fumbling in the closet, she found the steel case she kept her gun in. Where was the damn key?

The crash from downstairs made her jump. Giving

her head a shake, confused as to why she was having so much trouble staying awake, she stumbled to her dresser for the key. Setting the case on the dresser, she rifled through her underwear drawer until she found the key. It took her several tries before she managed to unlock it. She drew in a deep breath, then pulled the gun from the case. She loaded it, her fingers not working like she wanted them to. She stumbled to her door, opened it and her eyes slanted against the light from the living room.

She heard grunts, swearing, and deduced it was coming from two males. Two men were in her home.

They came to rape her.

Beth panicked, her legs shaking, her hands quivering. She was frozen to her spot.

"Give it up, Justin. You can't beat me."

"Justin?" Beth called out, her words slurred.

"Run, Beth!" Justin screamed at her, kicking her instincts in gear. But instead of running, she took a step down. He was in trouble; she could hear that even though her brain was foggy. She needed to help him. She needed to protect him.

She stepped down and saw in a blur, two men fighting. "Freeze," she called out, hating how drunk her words sounded.

Through burry eyes, she saw Wes when he turned. Her body shook, and she remembered how he had thrown her to the couch, how he'd ripped her shirt open, how he'd tried to force himself on her.

Then she saw the gun.

"Drop your weapon," she called out, gripping the barrel tight.

"Fuck you."

He raised his hand and Beth squeezed the trigger.

~

"What a day," Vic said, taking the beer Tom handed him.

"You can say that again." Tom sat beside Vic, his own beer in hand. "You're not going to stop Beth from getting away, are you?"

"Do you have to ask?" One look at his friend and he got the answer. "Hell no, Tom. Come on, you know me better than that."

"I just had to make sure."

"I was there when she came in. I saw what condition she was in. She tried to be brave but she was shaking like a leaf. I'd have to be a pretty shitty superior, not to mention a rotten godfather, if I refused her leave."

Tom nodded, drew in a breath before speaking. "So what do you think of our kids getting together?"

"Kinda weirds me out," Vic admitted with a smile. "We used to let them play naked in the pool together."

"When they were toddlers."

"Shoulda figured it was bound to happen, though. They were practically inseparable."

"You think it'll last?"

Vic shrugged, lighting a cigarette. "Guess time will tell."

"If this bastard isn't caught within the week, I'm hiring a private investigator."

"Gee, nothing like having faith in your friend." Vic sneered.

"I trust your investigative abilities, but you can only do so much, a P.I. can work twenty-four seven. She's my baby, Vic."

"I know, pal, I know." Laying a reassuring hand on his friend's shoulder, Vic nodded. When his radio went off, Vic pulled it from his pocket and answered in hopes that Wes had been found. "Davis."

"Vic, we just got a call. Shots were fired at Beth's house."

Tom was up in a flash and Vic recited his orders as he ran after his friend. "You're staying here, Tom."

"The hell I am."

Vic blew out an exasperated growl as his friend tore off in his truck.

~

"Put down the gun, Beth," Justin said calmly. She had a blank look in her eyes that worried him. "Sweetie, let me have the gun."

"No," she blurted out, shaking her head. "If you touch it, it'll have your prints on it. I have to check him—"

"You have to put the gun down first," he pleaded with her. She looked dazed, and he wondered how much of it was shock and how much was drug-induced.

She shook her head, lowering her weapon. "I have to check if he's okay."

"Beth—"

"I'm okay," she insisted, then drew in a deep breath. "It's part of my job, Justin. I have to do this." Taking the last step down, Beth hurried to Wes, kneeling by his side.

She wasn't in her right mind, because if she were, she wouldn't have brought the gun with her when she checked Wes out. Now it was his turn to help her.

Kneeling down beside her, Justin took the gun from her hand.

"What are you doing?"

"Helping you."

"Your fingerprints will be on the gun. Damn it, Justin."

"Your mind is foggy, Beth. Probably the drugs in your system. Think about it. You just knelt down to check Wes for vitals. Holding the gun. What if he jumped you and turned it on you?"

"He's not going to be doing that," she stated. "He's dead."

Justin looked down through swollen eyes and saw the bullet wound to Wes' chest. Right over his heart. The room went just a little screwy on him.

"Sit down. Jesus, look at you. Your face looks like it was beaten with a meat tenderizer."

"Pretty close." When she put her arm under his to help him up, he winced. "Think my ribs might look like my face."

"I heard something in my sleep." She sat him on the sofa. "I thought someone was breaking in. I knew I needed my gun, I knew I needed to protect myself, but my mind was so…foggy."

"The sleeping pill."

"Yeah. Give me the gun now, Justin."

"I don't want you having to take the rap for this. Let me do it. I'll tell my father I used your gun for self-defense."

"Oh, Justin." She touched his swollen face. "Don't be a dolt." Then pulled the gun from his hand, much to his surprise. Grabbing the corner of her robe, she wiped it clean.

"Why the hell did you do that?"

"My prints will be the only ones on the gun. I'll be brought up before the board. I'll have to answer questions about tonight and I'll tell the truth. At most, I'll receive a suspension. You, on the other hand, would go to jail. I am not letting you go now that I finally have you, so stop trying to be heroic."

He heard the sirens in the distance and knew they'd run out of time. "I love you, Elizabeth Healy. Did you know that?"

"I do now."

Epilogue

Who knew he would actually enjoy living in Passion again? He'd been a resident for nearly seven months now. He still traveled to Mississauga to check on his bar, which was in Sara's very capable hands. But for the most part, he lived in Passion.

There hadn't been much discussion about him moving in with Beth. It just sort of happened. After the incident with Wes, after Beth had killed him, Justin hadn't wanted to leave her side. There had been an investigation, just like she'd said, but in the end the board had deduced she'd used her weapon accordingly. She'd feared for her life when Wes had raised his gun. Plus she'd been protecting a civilian.

Justin had done as he'd promised, and taken her away for a week. She'd seen a shrink, dealt with her ordeal, and she was coping with it as per norm. She still had the occasional nightmare, but Justin was always right there to hold her and comfort her.

In the seven months since he'd moved in with her, they'd rarely been apart. And Justin was going to see to it that they never were.

The restaurant he'd had built for his mother had come together flawlessly, and while it was being constructed, Justin took great pleasure in watching his mother's excitement grow. She deserved to have this, and so much more.

He'd planned it perfectly, having the grand opening

on New Year's Eve, not just to welcome his new business into a new year, but to start a new life, as well.

A new life with Beth.

Once upon a time he couldn't fathom being with only one woman for the rest of his life. Now, he couldn't imagine not being with her.

As the clock inched towards midnight, Justin gave the nod to his crew and waited while they handed out fresh glasses of champagne. He took the two handed to him and held one out to Beth who stood at his side.

Everyone from town had shown up, his entire family was here, as were the Healys. It truly was the perfect moment.

"Could I have everyone's attention please? People, hello…" Beth put her fingers to her lips and whistled so loud, it rang in his ears. "Thanks, dear." He looked over the crowd whose attention he now had. "First, I would like to thank everyone for joining us in the grand opening of Julia's. Beginning January second, you all will be treated on a daily basis to the wonderful cuisine of the best cook in the world." His mother's face turned red, but he spoke the truth. "And if it's a drink you want after a long day's work, or hanging with your friends, Vic's Lounge is the place for you. But before we raise our glasses in a toast, I would like to thank a few people, because without them, I wouldn't be who I am today."

He took a deep breath and began. "To my father, for riding my ass and welcoming me back with open arms. To my mother, for pushing me away and knowing it was the right thing to do. To Beth, for making me see the light." He turned to her with a smile. "And lastly, to my late grandfather Leo. Without his persistence and guidance, none of this would be possible. So raise your glasses now, and toast not just the opening of a great restaurant and lounge, but to a new beginning."

He waited while everyone held their glasses up, then held his up before bringing it to his lips. Out of the corner of his eye, he watched Beth. When it hit her lip, and she pulled the glass away, he turned to her. "Is there something wrong with your wine, sweetie?"

Her brow curled as she looked into the glass. "There's something in it."

"What? Let me see." Titling her glass, he bit his lip when he looked inside. "Well, you're right, there is. Let me see what it is." Dipping his fingers inside the bubbly, he pulled the object out. "Hmm, it appears to be a ring."

Beth gasped, her eyes meeting Justin's in wide-eyed astonishment.

"I wonder how it got in there—oh, wait," he met her eyes. "I put it there." Because he wanted to do this with as much tradition as possible, he got down on one knee, holding the ring out to Beth.

The room went absolutely still.

"Elizabeth Healy, will you do me the honor of becoming my wife?"

Her mouth fell open and her hands began to shake. "Is this for real?"

Laughing, Justin took her left hand in his, then pinched it. "It's for real."

"Oh, my God, Justin!"

"Is that a yes, or a no?" She was killing him.

Her head bobbed up and down rapidly. "Yes, yes, oh, God, yes."

The overhead lights caught the diamond as he slipped it onto her finger, creating a kaleidoscope of color that sparkled on her hand. As he stood, the crowd let out a roar of applause. He took her into his arms, looking into her beautiful blue eyes. "I love you with all my heart, Beth, and I am going to do my best to make you happy for the rest of our lives."

As he took her lips and sealed the promise, fireworks exploded in the night sky.

A new year was upon them. A new life was just beginning.

The End

About the Author:

Shiela Stewart has been writing for the better part of twenty years, pouring her heart out in words, living a fantasy through the characters she creates. It has always been a dream of hers to have her work published, a dream she has finally seen come to life.

When not writing, she is busy working on two websites for organizations she belongs to, tending to her three children, and spending time with the love of her life, William.

Shiela has a deep affection for animals and it's evident in the five cats, one dog, eight fish, and three turtles she owns. Aside from writing, she enjoys sketching, painting, singing, and dancing, as well as stargazing, astronomy, and astrology. Her favorite time of the day is sunset.

Also by Shiela Stewart:

Kidnapped

Elizabeth Cromwell is rich, gorgeous and doesn't have a care in the world. Until she's whisked away in a van, blindfolded and gagged. Liz is helpless and completely unable to fight against her abductor. Or so he thinks.

Mackenzie Tyrell is a good man in a desperate situation. About to see all of his hopes and dreams die, Mac gets caught in a web of deceit that may become his undoing.

The plan was simple—abduct the beautiful blonde and hold her for ransom. But when the feisty Elizabeth escapes and then turns the table on Mac, all bets are off. Now he's tied up and at Liz's mercy. Was this the worst mistake Mac's ever made? Or, will the choice lead him to discover something and someone that will change his life forever?

Kidnapped by Shiela Stewart is full of suspense and steeped in sensuality. This fast-paced novel is guaranteed to hold you hostage until the very last page.

Secrets of the Dead

Jessica Coltrane is a die-hard skeptic who believes that ghosts and paranormal activity are nothing more than a figment of some poor fool's over active imagination—until she finds herself locked inside a house with the enigmatic paranormal investigator C.J. Dowling, that is.

C.J., born with the ability to see and speak to the dead, thought this would be a job like many others. Calm and self-assured, he knows his business. After all, he's been listening to the *Secrets of the Dead* since he was three. He's prepared for anything—except the smart and sexy Jessica.

Working together in close quarters, C.J. and Jessica find it's all too easy to get under one another's skin during the day. As darkness falls and the tension between them mounts, a spark is ignited. Fueled by passion they give into their desires...only C.J. and Jessica aren't alone.

As the light dawns the couple discovers they're trapped. Trapped with the ghost of a child long forgotten, an amorous entity that is threatening Jessica, and a powder keg of a spine-tingling mystery that might just be better left buried.

Discovery in Passion

Book One of the Passion Series

Nothing is ordinary in the small town of Passion, especially the love.

Wanting to start fresh, Cassie Evans relocates to the small town of Passion where she moves into the home of her dreams, complete with dreamy next door neighbor, artist, and handyman Thomas Healy. The only problem is, the house she bought just might be haunted.

Thomas Healy lives a life of solitude and that suits him just fine. Then Cassie Evans moves in next door and begins to turn his peaceful live upside down. He tries to ignore her, but ignoring a woman as beautiful as Cassie isn't so easy, especially when she shows up at your door, naked, begging for you to paint her. Thomas' first mistake was to agree to it, his second was to take Cassie to bed, now she's all he can think about.

When their blossoming love is overshadowed by a ghostly haunting, the curious Cassie launches an investigation into the life and death of her home's previous owner, uncovering a mystery and attracting the attention of a killer. Where will Cassie's discovery lead her, to the love of her life or to death itself? Welcome to the town of Passion.

Escape in Passion

Book Two of the Passion Series

Nothing is ordinary in the small town of Passion, especially the love.

Victor Davis is a man trying to escape the tragedy of his past. Several months ago, a bullet that was meant for him killed his girlfriend by mistake. Now struggling to move on, Victor's taken over as the chief of police of Passion. Vic knows everyone in Passion, so naturally he can't help but notice when beautiful stranger Julia Wilson moves into the small town.

Mysterious and alluring, Julia came to Passion with one thing on her mind, avenging the death of her sister. Desperate to find the truth, and keeping her true identity a secret, Julia enters into an affair with the one man she thinks might be able to give her answers—Victor Davis.

Lust and love run rampant when Victor and Julia enter into a torrid romance. But Julia's deception turns dangerous and secrets from Victor's past soon threaten their fragile relationship. Murder, kidnapping, and an escape that you'll never forget. Welcome to the town of Passion.

This is a publication of
Linden Bay Romance
WWW.LINDENBAYROMANCE.COM

Recommended Read:

Forbidden: The Revolution
by Samantha Sommersby

Experience the magic...

Twenty-five years ago Dell Renfield's father started a revolution. Dell plans to finish it. Sorcerer, sexy vampire, secret weapon, he's spent his entire life training for what he believes to be his fate. The one deterrent he isn't equipped for? Special Agent Alexandria Sanchez.

Alex is quick-witted, hot-tempered, and strikingly beautiful. Normally focused on getting the job done, she's completely unprepared for her new partner, Dell, and his mysterious ability to drive her to distraction.

Posing as lovers, Alex and Dell infiltrate a dangerous culture where the macabre seems mundane and passion is power. Unable to deny their attraction or resist temptation they begin a journey, entering into a torrid affair that will forever change their destiny.

An age-old secret, a consort held hostage, a curse demanding to be broken, and an unforgettable battle with a mercenary master mage will have you holding your breath. Let Samantha Sommersby lead you into a world like no other, a world where vampires are real, where magic is possible, and where love still conquers all.

Indulge in the *Forbidden*, because sometimes giving in to temptation can be a good thing.

Made in the USA